Out of Order

Geoff Lambton

Michael Terence
Publishing

First published in paperback by
Michael Terence Publishing in 2021
www.mtp.agency

Copyright © 2021 Geoff Lambton

Geoff Lambton has asserted the right to be identified as the
author of this work in accordance with the
Copyright, Designs and Patents Act 1988

ISBN 9781800942400

No part of this publication may be reproduced, stored in
a retrieval system, or transmitted, in any form or by
any means, electronic, mechanical, photocopying,
recording or otherwise, without the prior
permission of the publishers

Cover images
Copyright © Aridha Prassetya, Khoon Lay Gan
www.123rf.com

Prologue

Twenty-Two Years Ago

'Twice as many people are killed by vending machines every year than are killed by sharks.'

This raised a few questions in the mind of the young man driving the car, the first one being whether it was true or not. These people must be experts, so for the moment he would assume it was true. He was young and naive. Later in life, when he was older and wiser, he would not be so eager to believe everything so-called experts told him.

The next thing he wondered was how many people that actually was. Were they talking dozens? Or even hundreds? He had no idea. But the biggest puzzle was how a vending machine could actually kill somebody.

The most obvious thing he could think of was someone pulling a machine over while tilting it to try and steal some chocolate and getting crushed. He'd had to repair the damage of such attempts often enough. The other possibility was being poisoned. He had seen the inside of enough coffee machines to know that wasn't out of the question. Or maybe some of them had brought on heart attacks by getting so angry because a machine hadn't given them their correct change, although technically that could be classified as self-inflicted rather than the vending machine doing the killing. Later in his career he would discover this was not as far-fetched as it seemed now.

Neither would be vending machine related murders, but again that wouldn't really be the vending machine doing the killing.

But the most important question to him was how many of the victims of vendicide were customers trying to buy stuff, and how many were engineers trying to repair a broken machine. This was important because he didn't like the idea of being killed in the line of duty. He didn't get the answer to many of his questions. The programme was all about sharks, not vending machines. The host was concentrating on defending sharks, and had eventually mentioned that there were only four deaths from shark attacks worldwide in the previous year, which was one fewer than the annual average. Therefore, a quick calculation suggested ten people were killed on average every year by vending machines. He turned the radio off and put a CD on instead.

Cecil Barnard had only been in the job for three months. He'd never worked before. It was a real wakeup call from the life he'd known as a student. Student life in a hall of residence in London was four years of partying. He and his friends spent most evenings getting as drunk as possible, then doing just enough work to scrape through the exams at the end of the year. But as it happened Cecil more than scraped through. He passed his Electrical and Electronic Engineering degree more comfortably than he could have expected given that he'd spent most of those years drinking beer, chasing girls, and watching bands. The downside was it was an expensive lifestyle, especially for someone who didn't have much money.

Out of Order

After he graduated, he never quite landed the job he imagined he would. He had applied to various companies, and had a few interviews. He wasn't very successful at interviews. It didn't help that he didn't really know what he wanted to do, so he found it difficult to convince any companies he was serious about wanting the job.

He had taken a job with a vending machine company called Hot Cup. They'd advertised for engineers, and he thought it would be good enough for a while until he found his dream job. But he had no idea what that dream job was, other than being a professional darts player, or playing cricket for England. Working for a living was never something he'd considered having to do.

After a few weeks he was finding it quite enjoyable. For a start they gave him a car, with petrol, road tax, insurance, and servicing all paid for. He was also given a mobile phone and a uniform. These things were all very handy to someone who'd spent four years building up a large overdraft.

But the thing he liked most about the job was that he didn't have to stay in the same building all day. He found it hard enough to stay awake during the afternoon lectures at university. He doubted he would be able to survive working in an office every day. But in this job, if he started feeling drowsy, he could just park somewhere quiet and have a quick nap. Which he did occasionally, especially when he'd had a big drink on the previous evening. After a few weeks in this job, he decided this was just right for him. He'd been sent to repair machines in places that made the job sound glamorous. He'd been in the

Tower of London, the Bank of England, the Stock Exchange, Madame Tussauds, London Zoo, Twickenham Rugby Stadium, the Hilton, the Ritz, Harrods, and the BBC. He'd also been up to the tops of the NatWest Tower and Canary Wharf. He'd even been in the Houses of Parliament, where he had to show a struggling MP how to get a cup of coffee out of a machine.

But little did he know, it wasn't going to turn out to be the cushy life he thought it was going to be. His engineering degree wasn't going to cut as much ice as he assumed it would out there in the big bad world.

The three months had gone well enough. He hadn't had to do anything too difficult. Just the odd tricky moment. He found the customers he had to deal with friendly enough, but he did think people tended to get a bit too worked up because their vending machine had gone wrong. It wasn't proportional to real life. He had seen it happen.

'Hello. I'm here to repair your photocopying machine.'

'Oh hi. Take a seat. Would you like a coffee while you wait? We weren't expecting you until a week on Tuesday.'

Or alternatively.

'Hello. I'm here to repair your vending machine.'

'About bloody time. We've had no coffee for ten minutes. Your company is useless.'

The worst aspect of the job, or so he thought at this early stage in his career, was the traffic in London. It wasn't too bad during the day, and he was generally making short journeys between jobs. But the journeys in and out of the city during morning and evening rush hours could be horrendous. He was OK with it at first. He would just put on some loud music and switch off from his surroundings. What really frustrated him most was the awful standard of driving. It seemed to him all the worst traits of human behaviour were brought out in car drivers. Laziness, inconsideration, stupidity, an inability or unwillingness to follow rules. Worst of all aggression. Drivers lost their tempers way out of proportion for little things that have upset them. It wouldn't be long before he discovered vending machines could induce the same symptoms in the people who used them. But he managed to put up with it for ten years before moving to an area with quieter roads and less stressed motorists.

The job Cecil had been sent to today was to repair a carbonator unit, which was a cold drinks dispenser that gave out orange and blackcurrant chilled drinks, either fizzy or still. The reported fault was that the blackcurrant wasn't dispensing. It wasn't a problem that was going to bother someone of Cecil's technical ability. But as he was removing a connector which he assumed was the cause of the problem, a jet of blackcurrant syrup shot straight into his eye. He instinctively threw his head to one side, which allowed the jet of syrup to gush onto the lady who was unlucky enough to be walking past. Cecil had never heard anything like the reaction that followed. The recipient of the blackcurrant shower acted as if she'd been squirted with some deadly acid. She shouted some abuse that he thought was totally uncalled for, and way out of proportion for what she'd had to endure. This came as a bit of a shock to Cecil. And just to add to his woes, as he walked away from the building, he was surrounded by wasps attracted by the blackcurrant syrup all over his face and shirt, resulting in him running back to his car, shouting, and waving his arms around while people stared.

Cecil, being fairly new to the job had a lot to learn. He was making his way in the world. He wasn't confrontational by nature. He wasn't the sort who wanted to argue with anybody. But this was an eye opener for him. Should he be getting abuse hurled at him when all he was doing was his job? Was that how the world was? What kind of response would he get if he reported it to his employers? He was soon going to find out the answer to that one.

A few days later he was sent to do another job which didn't go too well either. He went to fix a machine in an office. It should have been a straightforward job, just a routine descaling of a coffee machine. But the coffee machine was situated in an awkward place. There was no space for him to manoeuvre and there were people sitting around their desks who refused to move and looked at him like he was a piece of something you would wipe off your shoe. He couldn't help bumping into the back of one of the occupied chairs and was rewarded with some spiteful comments. If he'd been more experienced, he would have walked out and told them it wasn't feasible to carry out the work safely unless they moved. But he was new, eager to please, and tried his best to do the job. Then it went horribly wrong.

While he was pouring some descaling acid into the machine, some of it dripped onto a jacket hanging on the back of a chair. The man who'd been making a point of ignoring Cecil while hindering his ability to do his job had a tantrum a three-year-old would be proud of. He had to endure another torrent of abuse for the second time in a week.

The descaling acid was quite weak, and hadn't caused any real damage to the jacket. But it was enough to get the owner on the phone and make a complaint.

One of the things he liked best about the job was that he didn't have to see his bosses. Everything was done over the phone. He'd been to the head office in the London borough of Lambeth, just south of the river a few times when he first started, but now he was out on the road, he never needed to go there. So, he was surprised when his manager John Harris phoned him two days after the descaling job and asked him to come in. He didn't think anything of it. But he was soon to learn that being summoned to the office usually meant trouble.

The office was fairly close to the area he was covering in the West End, so he arrived there not too long after he was called. He went straight to the boss's office. He didn't know Harris all that well yet. He'd only known him for three months, and didn't feel comfortable with him. He took the job far too seriously in Cecil's opinion, and could do with lightening up a bit.

'Hello Cecil. Take a seat. How are you getting on out there?'

'Not too bad. I've had a couple of tricky jobs in the last few days. But in general, it's been going OK.'

But Harris soon dropped his phoney friendly act.

'I'm afraid we've had two complaints against you.'

'Why? What have I done?'

'Well, the first one was from a woman who said you squirted blackcurrant syrup all over her skirt and blouse.'

'It wasn't me who squirted her. It was a fault on the machine that caused it I didn't do anything wrong. Most of it hit me anyway.'

'That's not how she sees it. Then there's the other one. A man said you burnt a hole in his jacket with acid.'

Cecil tried to defend himself, but could see it wasn't going to work. Harris wasn't interested in his version of events.

'That wasn't my fault either. He refused to move and I had no space to do the job properly.'

'This is all part of the job. You need to learn how to handle the situation better.'

He didn't have an argument to respond with. So, he just took it on the chin. But he wasn't expecting what came next.

'We have been sent two bills. One for dry cleaning, and one for a new jacket. The cost of these will be taken from your wages.'

Cecil was stunned. Was he even allowed to do that? But again, he didn't have an answer.

He was told he could go, but as he was about to leave, Harris had something else he wanted to add.

'Oh, and one more thing. I had a look at your car. It's dirty. I won't tolerate that. You need to keep it clean.'

Out of Order

After the meeting was over, Cecil drove away in his car, which he didn't think looked too dirty at all. Why did it matter anyway? Nobody else cared how clean his car was. He felt bullied and disheartened. He could hardly afford to lose the money from his wages either. It wasn't going to help him pay off the overdraft he'd accumulated while he was a student.

Cecil couldn't face doing any more work after that. Apart from feeling angry, his legs were hurting. He'd been playing football at the weekend, and although he loved his football, it did cause him quite a bit of discomfort in the early part of the week. That was the one drawback of not having a desk job.

He went home to Maidenhead where he lived with his mum and dad. He had to move back in with them after leaving university until he could somehow afford a place of his own. It had been by far the worst day in his short working life. He never forgot it. And from that point onward he took a whole new approach to his work, and it completely changed how he interacted with customers and bosses.

1

Present day

Cecil Barnard and his son, also Cecil Barnard were at the Oval cricket ground, in London. It was the second day of a test match between England and New Zealand. The younger Cecil had bought his dad two tickets as a present for his 70th birthday which had been four days earlier.

It was just like the old days. They used to go to a lot of England games together at the Oval and Lords when Cecil was a young boy, but today was the first time they had done it for many years. The Oval had changed so much since those days. The iconic gas holders were still there, but a huge new stand had been built at the Vauxhall end of the ground, and there were new buildings at the Pavilion end too, mainly to accommodate corporate hospitality, because as in most high-profile sports, making money had become very important. But the ground still retained a lot of its old character. The tickets they had were for seats on the more traditional uncovered area sideways to the pitch, right at the front. They were happy with that. They didn't want to be high up in the sky watching through a window.

They took their seats half an hour before the start to give themselves time to soak up the atmosphere. The sun was shining and the crowd noise level was no more than a gentle buzz. It was pleasant at this time of the day before alcohol kicked in. Later on, the gentle buzz would be replaced by drunken chants, and an annoying git with a trumpet who seemed to follow the England cricket team everywhere they went, under the delusion everybody enjoyed his trumpet playing. And of course, there would also be the tedious Mexican wave.

It would appear they had picked the right day to come too. The game was perfectly poised. On the first day England had bowled New Zealand out for 245, and had scored 30 without loss before the close. If all went well, they could sit all day watching England bat and take control of the match.

However, it didn't get off to an ideal start. England lost a wicket in the second over and after twenty minutes the sunny skies had disappeared and it started to rain. It wasn't very heavy, but enough for the umpire to send the players back to the pavilion. The weather forecast had predicted the possibility of early showers which would soon clear away and it would be sunshine for the rest of the day.

They didn't want to get wet, so took a walk into one of the bars. While queuing at the bar, Cecil senior said, 'Hey look. Isn't that one of yours?'

Cecil junior looked at the coffee machine with the Vendetta logo and embarrassing slogan 'Refreshingly Simple' on the front. The younger Cecil worked for Vendetta as an Engineer. He'd been with them for twelve years and had worked in the vending machine industry for twenty-two years in total. He was well aware of his value to the company, and did what some of his work colleagues referred to as 'taking liberties'. They had a point. In fact, he was taking a big liberty today. When he requested a day off to go to the cricket, his boss had refused the request on the grounds that there were already too many engineers on holiday that day. Cecil wasn't going to be thwarted. He had phoned in on the morning to pretend that he was ill.

His dad asked the barman for a coffee.

'Sorry sir, our coffee machine isn't working at the moment. If you want a coffee you can get one at one of the other bars.'

Cecil junior said, 'Yes, that's one of ours alright. It's out of order. Not that it affects me. I'm having a lager.'

So, they bought a pint of lager and a half of bitter, and took them outside just in time for the sun to come out. They returned to their seats for the resumption of the cricket.

The sun was shining for the rest of the day, and the game progressed nicely. They had a few more beers and the occasional conversation.

'Thanks for getting the tickets. It was a great idea.'

'No problem.'

'Maybe I'll return the favour when you become 70.'

'That won't be for another 25 years.'

'It will come around sooner than you think.'

'That doesn't make sense. It'll come around when I'm expecting it to. In 25 years.'

'Alright smartarse. You know what I mean.'

'Yeah, OK. Well, I've always wanted to go to the Grand National. You could get me tickets for that.'

'I doubt I'll be capable of travelling to Liverpool when I'm 95.'

From that day Cecil was determined to go to the Grand National for his 70th birthday celebration in 25 years' time, no matter how soon it came around.

England batted well and matched the New Zealand score for the loss of five wickets just before the tea interval. Cecil junior had a moment of glory when the ball was hit straight to where he was sitting. It hit the boundary rope and popped up over the advertising board, straight into his hands. He had played a fair bit of cricket when he was younger, and he made the catch look easy, even though it had some pace on it and he had to stretch. But throwing was never his strong point, so he executed a gentle underarm throw to lob the ball back to the New Zealand fielder who had come to retrieve it. The ball didn't reach him and plopped weakly onto the grass in front of him.

During the tea break Cecil's phone rang. The name Liam appeared on the screen. Liam was one of the other Vendetta engineers. He answered in faked irritation.

'Yes? Can I help you?'

'Alright Barney? How's it going?'

'Liam. What the hell are you calling me for? You know I'm off work sick.'

'Don't give me any of that bollocks!' replied Liam. 'You've already told me you were going to the test match.'

'In that case that's even worse disturbing me while I'm at the test match. This had better be important.'

'I want your advice on a snack machine I'm having trouble fixing. Oh, and I think I've just seen you on the television.'

'What? How?'

'I'm in a staff canteen of one of our customers. They've got the cricket on, and I'm sure it was you that threw the ball back. Quite pathetically I might add.'

'Yes, that was me. You must admit the catch was good though. What's your problem with the vending machine?'

Liam explained his problem, and Cecil told him how to fix it. Something which happened quite often. He sometimes thought he ought to be getting a cut of Liam's wages. Then he had to hang up as the cricket was about to resume.

For a moment he felt quite chuffed he'd been on the television. He hoped his friends had seen him. But then something else occurred to him.

'Oh my god!' he exclaimed rather loudly.

'What's up?' his dad asked.

'I've just been spotted on the telly.'

'Oh. Nice one.'

'No, it isn't. It's not a nice one at all. My boss is a big cricket fan. He's got a TV in his office. He'll be watching.'

'What's wrong with that?'

'I'm not supposed to be here. I called in sick this morning.'

'That was a stupid thing to do. Why didn't you just book a day off?'

'Oh right, what a brilliant idea! Why on earth didn't I think of that?' he said in the biggest sarcastic tone he could muster.

'He might not have seen you.'

'I hope not. But even if he didn't, someone else at work could have seen it, and word gets around quickly at our place.'

Cecil senior could detect the irritation in his son's voice and knew from experience it was time to change the subject.

'Incidentally, how's your own cricket going these days,' he asked.

'I've given up playing.'

'Yes, I thought so. I could tell from the way you threw that ball back.'

'Very funny. I had to stop playing. My body couldn't take it anymore.'

'Too much beer. That's your problem.'

'I don't have a problem,' snapped his son.

The irritation had returned and his dad knew it was time to shut up.

Another hour passed and the game continued to go well. Then his phone rang again. The call he'd been dreading. The name 'Grumbling Bowels' flashed up on the screen. He knew that meant he was going to be in trouble.

2

'Good afternoon. Can I help you?'

'Hi. I'm from Vendetta. I'm here to repair your vending machine.'

The words he had repeated five or six times every working day for the past twenty-two years. During this time, he had learned to expect one of several standard responses. The most welcome one was along the lines of 'Oh wonderful. They'll be glad to see you'. Life would be so much easier if this happened every time. Sadly, it's more likely to be a less friendly greeting, such as 'about time! Or 'not again!' Or 'why don't you just move your bedroom here?', which was a phrase often used by people who thought they were hilarious and assumed they were the only ones who ever said it.

Sometimes instead of ridicule it could get quite nasty. 'Your machine is rubbish and your company is useless'. And on some occasions, they would even just respond by laughing at him. But Barney's favourite reaction was from the ones who were looking for an argument. Because he felt he was equipped with the ammunition to win most of the arguments. This often got him into trouble with his employers, because quite often after a customer had been made to look stupid, they would react by calling the company and making a complaint about the engineer.

On this particular occasion the customer was looking to take his frustrations out on someone and Barney took up the challenge.

Out of Order

The receptionist had called one of her colleagues who came to meet him, and escorted him to the vending machine. The man hadn't introduced himself, so Barney decided he would be called Adam, once he'd delivered his opening salvo which was, 'Your machine is infested with ants.'

To which Barney replied, 'It's not my machine.'

'Well, your company's machine then.'

'It's not my company's machine either. Your company bought the machine. So it's your machine.'

'Your company manufactured it.'

'No, they didn't, we don't manufacture machines.'

'I don't care about all that. What are you going to do about your ants?'

'They are not my ants. Or my company's ants. Nor do we manufacture ants. They got into the machine from your building. If they are anyone's ants, they are your ants.'

'I think you are being unnecessarily pedantic. What are you going to do about the ants?'

'Nothing. I'm an engineer, not a pest controller. Try calling Rentokil.'

'I don't like your attitude.'

'Why? I'm only giving you the facts. We can send someone else if you prefer. They could tell you the same thing using a different attitude.'

On that note he said his goodbyes to Adam and the ants and

left the building. He was fairly pleased, because he didn't think there would be any comeback as he was completely in the right. Although it didn't always work that way. He was also pleased to get the job out of the way quickly without having to do any actual work. His darts team had a match that evening, and he wanted to get away early.

His darts matches were the highlight of his week, and he liked to get home, get changed, leave the car, and catch a train into London to the pub. If ever he was held up at work, he would get irritable and it could affect his performance. But thanks to the ant episode he was going to knock off an hour earlier than he was supposed to. He climbed in the car and was about to set off for home. Then his heart sank when a message appeared on his screen.

Usually, a job coming in at this time could wait until the next morning, but this one came with an instruction from the regional manager Richard Bowles, who Barney had already had a few run-ins with. The instruction specified that the job was urgent and it must be completed today. He didn't say why it was urgent, but the usual reason for a call to be deemed urgent would be that an irate customer had phoned in and was ranting and demanding an immediate response. Under normal circumstances this would have had the opposite effect on Barney. He would deliberately take his time on his previous job, or go somewhere else to do a different job first. Then he could go home and come back in the morning to do the job. But because of the previous squabbles he'd had with Bowles there was no way he could ignore this. Fortunately, the customer was only two miles away from his previous one so he was at their reception within a few minutes.

'Good afternoon. How can I help you?'

'Hi. I'm from Vendetta. I'm here to repair your vending machine.'

'Oh. I don't know anything about it. And the lady who would normally deal with it has just popped out. She'll be back in twenty minutes. Would you like to take a seat and wait for her?'

Barney didn't want to sit around doing nothing for twenty minutes, or probably longer.

'Would it be OK for me to check out the machine while I'm waiting for her? I'm in a bit of a hurry.'

'Yes of course. No problem. By the way, I hope you don't mind me saying this, but I think you've got your shirt on inside out.'

He looked down at the badge and confirmed that indeed it was inside out. But at least that meant the embarrassing company slogan 'Refreshingly Simple' couldn't be seen. His excuse was that he got dressed in the dark that morning, although that didn't prevent him from feeling a bit silly. But the most baffling aspect of this was that he had met many other people throughout the day and not one of them had pointed it out. He didn't understand people. That was why he regularly found himself in trouble over his 'customer relations'.

Barney welcomed her friendly demeanour and helpfulness, in sharp contrast with the ant man. He thanked her for her help and popped into the gents to put his shirt on properly.

Something similar had happened to him once before. He had walked around for a whole day with a sock dangling down his back. It had got stuck on the Velcro on the hood of his jacket and he never spotted it when he put the jacket on. Again, on that occasion it must have been seen by many people throughout the day and not one of them mentioned it.

There have been other embarrassing moments for Barney during his career as a vending machine engineer. Like the time he was repairing a snack machine in the sixth form common room at an all-girls school near Guildford. He was attempting to carry out his work, surrounded by a group of flirty girls who wouldn't leave him alone and kept making comments to him. He tried to act as cool as possible, which shouldn't have been difficult. How can a 45-year-old man get so unnerved by a group of teenage girls? When he had completed the job, he walked away they all waved at him. He turned his head back towards them and gave a little wave back while simultaneously missing the doorway and thudding into the wall. The ensuing giggles still haunt him.

He quickly found his way to the vending machine, but what he found had the potential to deal an enormous blow to his darts match plans. The cause of the machine failing to cool was a faulty condenser fan motor. It would take about three quarters of an hour and a lot of effort and a covering of dirt all over his hands and clothes to fit a new one. He considered telling them he didn't have the required part and would have to order it and return tomorrow. But the problem with that plan was Bowles would be able to check on his computer what he was carrying in his car stock and if he discovered Barney was in possession of a fan motor he would be in yet more trouble. He'd already had a huge argument over his trip to the Oval. He denied going there, but the evidence on national television was stacked against him.

So, although he was desperate to get away, he reluctantly went to his car and dug out the new fan motor. Fortunately, the job went better than expected, and after thirty-five minutes he had the machine up and running again, just in time for the aforementioned lady to return and introduce herself. She was also very friendly. After Barney had explained to her what he had done, she said 'Oh, you needn't have bothered. The machine is getting removed tomorrow morning. It's getting replaced and the old one is being scrapped.'

He wanted to yell at the woman, even though she hadn't done anything wrong. But he managed to restrain himself. All he could manage was a feeble, 'Oh, great.'

Barney got in the car and hurried home to clean up. He was now running late and in a bad mood, and no doubt his performance at the darts would suffer this evening.

3

The train he had caught going to Paddington was an hour later than the one Barney had hoped to catch before he was sent to do the job that didn't need doing. If he'd caught the earlier train, he would have sat quite happily reading the newspaper, or looking out of the window at the passing landscape, and arrived at the darts match in a relaxed state of mind. It didn't help that the train kept coming to a standstill, and he was getting more and more agitated, especially with the repeated apologies being announced by the driver. 'Thank you for your patience' has to be the most pointless comment of all time. Why do they assume their passengers are being patient? Most of them are fed up sitting in a train that isn't going anywhere, and are desperate to get moving. Most of them have no patience whatsoever, and become even more impatient when they are thanked for their patience.

He was still feeling somewhat annoyed that he had wasted such a lot of unnecessary effort and used up so much time on that stupid job.

He wondered why had Bowles told him it was essential the job was done today. The only reason for that to happen would be that an angry customer had phoned up demanding someone attends to solve their problem immediately and were threatening to cancel the contract. But it certainly hadn't come from the customer on this occasion. They hadn't been expecting him and didn't care that their machine wasn't working. He suspected it was just an act of spite. He also suspected that there was another reason for this particular spite, which he was going to find out about in the near future. Bowles didn't like Barney very much, and the feeling was mutual. They'd had a few confrontations in the past following complaints from customers about Barney's attitude towards them. He held the view that the customer was always right, even when they were wrong. They had to be treated with courtesy at all times. If what they are saying is rubbish, humour them. Barney's view was rather different. He will treat people the way they treat him. If they are polite, he will be polite. If they are rude, he will respond accordingly. If they are talking rubbish, he will not hesitate to let them know.

The train eventually pulled into Paddington station and he headed towards the underground to catch a tube to Liverpool Street station. It was time to put work out of his head and focus on the darts match.

Barney enjoyed his darts evenings. His teammates were very good friends and they all liked a drink. They usually had a good laugh, but not always. Some of the opposition teams were less friendly than others, and it's amazing how controversial a game as simple as darts could be. He was expecting this evening to be even more enjoyable than usual. They were playing an away match against an opposition who were a friendly lot who didn't take it too seriously. They went by the name Norfolk and Good, which at first glance looks like a firm of solicitors, but when it's said out loud it takes on a whole new meaning.

Because he had caught the later train, he arrived just before the start of the match and the rest of his team, who went by the name of Mickey Mouse Club were already there. They mostly worked in the city, so didn't have far to travel to get there, and it looked like they had already got stuck into the beers. Roy, the team captain was at the bar getting a round in and asked Barney if he wanted a pint. On this occasion he accepted the offer, although he knew this meant that once he was part of the round, he was going to have a heavy night and would feel, and look horrible in the morning. More often than not he preferred to just buy his own drinks and go at his own pace, although that wasn't exactly slow either.

The game got started with a team leg, where all six players were involved and threw in turn. It was a bit of a warm up really, but still with a valuable point at stake. A point which went to Mickey Mouse Club. This was followed by six singles legs. Roy had put Barney down at number two, which he wasn't all that happy about because his late arrival had given him little time to relax, unwind, and have a few warm up throws. But Roy liked to do things his way and nobody ever questioned it. He had some unusual methods, but the general feeling among the team was that as he did all the organising, he could run things however he wanted, and everybody would respect that.

First up was Joe, who was generally recognised as the best player in the team. He was also the one who took it the most seriously. He won his leg without any trouble.

Then it was down to Barney to try to continue the perfect start. But he didn't exactly come flying out of the blocks. The first

Out of Order

three darts all went in the single 1. The first dart of his next visit also went in the 1, and his determination to avoid it happening again took both his next two darts into single 5. His next four visits were a sequence of increasingly better, but not great scores and he was soon put out of his misery by an average opponent.

Roy was always quick to try and console his players after they'd had a bad game. He came over to Barney, who was by now just finishing his third pint, and offered his customary 'Never mind lad. Better luck in the pairs.'

'Thanks,' said Barney, 'but I'm having one of those nights. I couldn't hit a cow's arse with a banjo. Scores of 3, 11, 26, 40, 41, 45 are not going to win you many games.'

'No. That's true. In fact, they look more like the winning lottery ticket numbers on a Saturday night.'

'Maybe I should buy a ticket with those numbers this weekend'

This gave Roy an idea. 'Why don't we have a lottery leg every week? We choose one particular game and take all the scores under 60 until we have six numbers. If we don't get six from that leg, it continues over to the next leg until we have six. Then we buy a ticket with those numbers at the weekend.'

Apart from Joe who thought it was a daft idea, the rest of the team were all for it, and spent the rest of the evening discussing ways to spend the winnings, one of which was to have a darts match in Las Vegas.

Barney was in need of such a windfall much more than the

others. The team never talked about their jobs much. Conversation mainly revolved around football, cricket, music, politics, and darts. But he knew that they all worked in city offices and banks, so were probably accountants or solicitors of some sort and no doubt earned more than a vending machine engineer. But they had no idea about the dire financial situation Barney was in. He had got himself deep into debt and owed a lot of money to some bad people.

They might have been given a bit of a clue if they'd watched him at the bar. When it was his turn to buy the round, his credit card was declined. It hadn't come as a huge surprise to him. It was something he knew had been coming and he had made sure he had enough cash in his pocket to cover it.

The match was eventually won by Mickey Mouse Club 8-3, and a lot more drinking followed, although this would have still been the case if they had lost. Barney hadn't contributed much. He didn't win his pairs match either and hadn't had a great day at all. The journey home was free from the delays of earlier, but it didn't make him feel any better. He had to somehow sort out his financial predicament. But he had no idea how he was going to do that.

4

The morning following a darts match was usually a big struggle for Barney. He was invariably tired, nauseous, and had a headache. All he wanted to do on a Friday was to get through the day with a minimum of effort and go home as early as possible. Today was no exception. It was a chilly and dull day, with a light sprinkling of rain, and a refreshing breeze, which were the ideal conditions when trying to recover from a hangover. Fortunately, he'd only been allocated one job so far this morning. Someone had reported that their coffee machine wasn't putting sugar in the drinks. He expected it to be an easy fix, although it didn't always work out that way.

The job was in the Slough Trading Estate, a place where he spent much of his working time. He parked his car outside an office and spotted a large white van with the Vendetta logo and embarrassing slogan 'Refreshingly Simple'. This instantly cheered Barney up as he knew it belonged to Alison, the vending operator, who's role was to fill and clean machines, collect cash, and report faults for engineers such as Barney to remedy.

He really liked Alison. She was from his generation, seven years younger at 38, and had similar contempt for the company's management and some of its customers. They would have a cup of tea together, swap stories about their latest exploits, and have a good moan about the company. But they always had a good laugh too. The only downside was they would have to take their drinks outside. Alison always needed a cigarette with her tea.

More than one. In fact, she smoked more than anyone else he had ever met.

Barney signed the visitors' book at the reception and went to the coffee machine. He knew where it was because he'd been here several times before. That was how he knew it was going to be a quick fix. This particular customer regularly reported trivial faults.

He found Alison next to the machine filling up the sugar container.

'Good morning Barney. You're looking a bit rough. Did you have one too many last night?'

'More than one too many.'

'Well, you'll be pleased to know I've already done your job for you. It had just run out of sugar. I've refilled it.'

'Don't give me that old cobblers. Refilling the sugar is your job, not mine.'

'Yes, but I know you. You'll make up some imaginary fault and claim to have fixed it.'

There was some truth to her accusation. One of the best things about this job was nobody could see what he'd done on a job, so his employers would have to believe whatever he told them. If he'd done a repair which took two minutes because some plonker had forgotten to plug the machine in, he could put down that it had a complicated electrical fault and took an hour and a half to rewire. Then he could go shopping, or to the pub, or sit in the car and read the newspaper. Or go home early.

'Oh, would I do such a thing?'

'Yes.'

'True. Shall we get a cup of tea and take it outside?'

'No. There's no need. I've given up smoking. I haven't had one for five weeks.'

Barney could have really done with going outside. The cool breeze and sprinkling of rain, along with a heavily sugared cup of tea were the ideal remedy for his hangover. But he needed to encourage Alison.

'Good for you. Are you still going to the gym?'

'Yes. I go most evenings as soon as I finish work. It's hard though. But I'm feeling so much better for it.'

Barney knew there were reasons behind her health regime. She'd had a tough time in recent years, but was on a path to what she hoped would be a better life.

He then told her that he had a feeling Richard Bowles was up to something and he was expecting a spot of bother. But he wasn't expecting it to happen quite so soon.

His phone rang and the name 'Grumbling Bowels' flashed up on his screen. He reluctantly pressed the answer button.

'Good morning Cecil. How are you?'

'Fine thanks,' Barney lied. He hated it when people called him Cecil, even though it was his name. And Bowles knew it.

'Would you mind coming into the office? We need to have a little chat.'

'What, right now?'

'Yes please. Once you've finished the job you're doing.'

'OK. Can I ask what it's about?'

'I'll tell you that when you get here.'

Oh, what a pain. It was bad enough having to go there any time. But with a hangover it was horrible. His regional depot was in Winchester, so it meant he had to make a round trip of over ninety miles, which he wasn't too keen on doing.

He had another cup of tea with Alison and said goodbye, then got in his car and set off to face whatever it was he was facing. Over the years he'd been summoned to the office several times, and it was usually because he'd rubbed somebody up the wrong way. He'd get a condescending lecture about how important 'customer relations' were, and get told not to do it again. He didn't ever take any notice. He would never forget that first time when he was a novice starting out at Hot Cup. It was a humiliating experience for someone so young and inexperienced. Now he was battle hardened and a lecture from the boss was water off a duck's back.

Barney had worked at Vendetta for twelve years. He joined them after he left Hot Cup under a cloud following an encounter with one of his customers. Most of his confrontations had at least some comedy value. This particular one wasn't funny in any way whatsoever.

In those days he was working in Central London. He'd been

assigned to repair a coffee machine in private surgery in Harley Street. Another engineer, a good friend of his and a more than capable engineer had been in there covering for Barney when he was on holiday. However, the man on site didn't share the same view about his colleague's ability.

'I'm glad you're back. That other guy they sent was useless.'

'Why, what did he do wrong?'

'He looked like he'd just swung down out of the trees.'

'What?'

'He looked like he'd just come out of the jungle, if you know what I mean?'

Barney knew exactly what he meant. But he had no intention of making things easy for him.

He said, 'No. I don't know what you mean. Please explain it to me.'

The man said nothing. He had realised he hadn't got the reaction from Barney he had been expecting.

Then Barney forced the issue.

'Are you trying to tell me he was black?'

The man opted for sarcasm.

'Oh no, no, no. You aren't allowed to say that these days, are you?'

Barney picked up his tool bag and started walking towards the door. The man shouted after him.

'What about my coffee machine?'

Barney turned around and walked up to the man until he was staring at him squarely in the face.

'You can shove your coffee machine up your arse!'

That exchange had resulted in a disciplinary meeting. He had joined a union several years earlier and a union rep came to the meeting with him. The rep was very good at his job and tied John Harris in knots. This was the same boss that had taken money from his wages, and lectured him about his car being dirty, all those years ago. He wasn't at all supportive of Barney over this latest incident, but he wouldn't dare sack him for it. As it involved blatant racism, the boss knew it meant Barney could cause embarrassment for the company if they took any action against him. A view enforced by the union rep. So, Harris was forced to absolve Barney from any blame.

The problem was Harris never forgave him for it, and when redundancies came around six months later, he was the first one out of the door.

He arrived at the office just before noon. Richard Bowles greeted him with a handshake, which he found quite creepy. He was taken to a meeting room where a lady he hadn't met before was sitting with some sort of notepad and pen at the ready. She was there to silently write down everything that was said. Even though he'd been through this sort of meeting several times before, this was only the second time someone was in with them writing it all down.

The previous time was when one of his customers phoned up complaining that Barney had implied that he was stupid. But it was the truth. The customer was stupid. A five-year-old could have made him look stupid. He had made himself look stupid all by himself with no help from Barney. But the outcome of it all was a verbal warning. Which meant this was potentially more serious than he had been anticipating.

Bowles started off, 'Thank you for coming. I just need to get a legal obligation out of the way first. I am required to tell you have the right to have a solicitor, union rep, or work colleague sitting in on this meeting, although they wouldn't be allowed to say anything.'

This got Barney wound up straight away.

'Well, it's a bit late telling me that now. Shouldn't you have given me prior notice so I could have arranged for someone to be here?'

'Technically yes. You have a right to request we postpone this meeting. But I'd rather we didn't have to. I could do without wasting any more time.'

Barney felt the need to be assertive. 'I need to think about this. I'm going outside to phone my union rep.'

He really wanted to get this out of the way today, whatever it was. He had enough worries with loan sharks breathing down his neck. If he had to come all the way back here for a rearranged meeting, it would just cause him more stress.

He didn't actually phone anyone and decided to bluff his way through. He let them wait a while, then went back inside and attempted to appear confident.

He started with a lie.

'I've just spoken with someone at my union. He has advised me to go ahead with whatever it is we're doing, but to take a copy of the notes that are made. Also, he has advised me that I can call a halt to proceedings at any time and walk out, then I would have a right to request a rescheduling of the meeting.'

He didn't know if any of this was true, but guessed they didn't know either.

Bowles didn't react to this. Instead, he came straight to the point.

'We have had a complaint from a customer about your behaviour at their site. We have brought you here to give you a chance to put your side of the story. '

Barney assumed that the ant man Adam had put in a complaint. It was hardly worthy of a complaint, but these people tend to enhance their story with exaggerations and even blatant lies. As it happened it wasn't about the ants.

'You have been accused of swearing at someone.'

'You'll have to be more specific.'

'So, you've done it more than once then?'

'No. I can't think of ever doing it at all.'

Which was true. He never used bad language if he could help it when dealing with customers. It handed them extra ammunition.

'You have been accused of shouting "shit" in their office quite loudly.'

It was at this point that he realised this was the same customer responsible for his previous verbal warning.

'Oh that. I was fixing their coffee machine when I accidentally touched my arm against the boiler. It hurt like hell. There's the burn mark still on my arm. I shouted "shit" as a reaction to the pain. It wasn't intentional. It wasn't aimed at anyone.'

'Well, they aren't happy about it.'

'Why not? I wasn't swearing at them. And are you trying to tell me an office full of adults and spotty adolescents are offended by such a mild word? It's a good job I never said anything a bit stronger. Would that have upset them a whole lot more? No, it wouldn't. The problem here is they just don't like me because I made one of them look stupid previously and it brings some satisfaction to their sad lives to get some kind of revenge.'

'You're not making this easy.'

'How? By not admitting I've done anything wrong, when I haven't done anything wrong?'

'Quite frankly I don't care whether you did anything wrong or not. I want you to go back there and apologise to them.'

'Not a chance. I'd rather be sacked. They should be apologising to me for not getting their first aider to treat my burnt arm. You apologise to them if you want. I'm not.'

'In that case you leave me no choice. Cecil Barnard, I am formally issuing you with a written warning about your future conduct. I must stress this is not a trivial matter. If there is any repeat of this sort of behaviour then your continued employment at the company will be in jeopardy. Do you understand?'

'Yes. I understand what your words mean. I don't understand why you're saying them. Do you seriously believe I'm in the wrong here?'

'You've had your warning. Don't be a fool. Nobody likes to see anyone lose their job.'

Barney didn't believe that for one minute. Bowles would love to see him lose his job.

On the drive home he considered the events of the meeting. Had he pushed him too far? He hadn't expected a written warning. Bowles wouldn't dare sack him. He was one of their best engineers. Or would that not count for anything to someone like him?

It was raining heavily now and the drive home was slow. His hangover had cleared up, but he was feeling miserable.

5

During a sleepless night Barney had done a lot of thinking. He was never going to conform for the likes of Bowles. He was never going to put on phoney politeness to people who didn't deserve it. It's not as if he went out and deliberately looked for confrontation. He just had a strong belief that everyone is entitled to carry out their job without being subject to snide remarks, ridicule and even abusive comments. And most importantly he felt that the company should defend their employees in such situations instead of making grovelling apologies and issuing written warnings.

On the other hand, he was in a perilous situation moneywise and losing his job would be a disaster. Maybe he had little choice. Would it be wise to rein himself in a little? Play their game for a while.

Very soon he was about to find out what an enormous challenge that was going to be.

Because he hadn't managed much sleep, he was in no mood to go rushing to get to work. It was a pleasant sunny morning. He visited his favourite cafe and took his time over a bacon sandwich and mug of tea while reading the newspaper and doing the crossword.

He'd started the day with a couple of routine easy fixes on coffee machines for customers he got on well with. Lots of friendly 'good mornings' and 'thank you for coming so quick.' Which was fine. He had no problems with people like that. He would go out of his way to help people who treated him respectfully. But doing good things never got reported to the bosses. They only heard the bad things. Nobody ever phoned Richard Bowles and said, 'I'm just calling to tell you what a superb job your engineer has done for us. The vending machine is brilliant and your engineer was polite and helpful, and never once tried to make me look like a total prick.'

Then he was asked to go and repair a water cooler at a place he'd never been before. But that shouldn't be much of a problem. There's nothing too complicated about water coolers. Not compared to human beings. It was going to be one of those days where he hoped the humans stayed out of his way and allowed him to do battle against the machines.

He was taken to the machine, which had a huge 'out of order' sign stuck to it. The young man who had escorted him asked if Barney would mind if he asked him a question.

He started off as usual in helpful mode.

'Of course you can. Fire away.'

'Why is the water in this machine cold?'

'Because it's a water chiller.'

'But I don't like chilled water. I like water at room temperature.'

'Then you shouldn't drink out of this machine.'

'Why not?'

'Because it's a water chiller.'

'Well, that's stupid.'

Barney was quite pleased when the man walked away. Perhaps that was the best way to deal with these situations. Say as little as possible, let them have their little moment and move on. Someone with that man's logic couldn't be reasoned with, so why get stressed about it?

No sooner had he got the machine working when a woman approached him. She was about to provide a sterner test. She'd apparently mistook him for someone who was trying to get a drink. She stood there staring for a while looking as if she was about to say something. Barney was getting irritated and spoke first.

'Yes?' He snapped.

She said, 'Can't you read?'

'Yes, I can read just fine,' he answered.

'Then there must be something wrong with your eyesight?'

'Not that I know of.' he replied.

'Then I think we'll have to get a bigger sign.'

'Oh, do you mean this thing?'

He then coolly pulled the sign off, scrunched it into a ball and threw it across the room where it landed in a rubbish bin, with a deadly accuracy that would have impressed his darts team mates. He turned to her and said 'My eyesight doesn't appear to be too bad. How's yours?'

At this point she saw his uniform and tool bag, realised her mistake, and her face turned a shade of purple.

So that wasn't too bad either. Making someone who thinks they're funny look really stupid without expending any energy. Let them do all the work.

But it didn't end there. What happened next made him begin to wonder if this job wasn't just a big prank on a hidden camera show for TV.

He had packed away his tools and was about to leave when a cleaner came in and started mopping the floor around him, leaving him stranded on a tiny island of floor in the middle of the room which she hadn't mopped yet. Sensing an aggressive mood, he didn't dare walk across the bit she had just mopped. She was chuntering away in a language he didn't recognise, and he didn't think she spoke English very well, but he guessed from her expression that she must have been unhappy that he was in the room while she was cleaning. Either that, or someone else from Vendetta had previously upset her and she was taking it out on him. He couldn't stand there any longer, so the only option was to walk over her clean floor. But before he could move, she mopped right across his shoes before picking up her bucket and storming out.

Barney could have probably picked up her bucket and tipped the contents all over her head and gotten away with it, given that she would have struggled to make herself understood when she reported him, but it was probably better that he hadn't. In fact, he felt quite amused by the whole thing.

So, no harm done there. He even got his shoes cleaned for free. He walked back to his car feeling satisfied. Had he turned over a new leaf? Maybe. But there was soon to be an encounter with someone that would threaten to tear his new leaf to shreds.

Out of Order

It was his last call of the day and by now he was feeling tired. The sleepless night was catching up on him. The receptionist looked like she'd also had a long and boring day, and he sensed she was in a bit of a mood. Which was understandable. It must get tedious sitting behind a desk all day long, putting on a fake smile and saying, 'Good afternoon, can I help you?' a hundred times.

She said exactly those words to him, but without the fake smile. She'd used up all her fake smiles on more important visitors.

'Hello, I'm from Vendetta. I'm here to repair your vending machine.'

'We haven't got a vending machine.'

'Oh. I must be in the wrong place. I'll just check the address.'

He went through the motions of checking the address, but needn't have bothered. He knew he was in the right place.

'Yes, this is the address I was given.'

'Are you sure you've got the right company?'

'Yes. If your sign above the door is correct.'

'Yes. It is.'

'I'll ring my company and see if I can get any more information, and see if I can find out the name of the person who called us.'

Barney phoned Mary, his customer help desk service coordinator, or Sweary, as the engineers referred to her. She was one of the few people at work who was entertaining to talk to and helped the day go by easier. Not that she ever swore at customers. She was all sweetness and niceties to them. A true professional. She just swore at the engineers, and her friends.

He explained the situation to her. She suggested helpfully, 'Oh just tell her to fuck off, Barney.'

Which sounded very tempting, but wouldn't have been the best thing to do, now that he was on a written warning.

But she did confirm the call details. They definitely had one of Vendetta's machines and someone had phoned in the fault just two hours ago.

He returned to the receptionist.

'Our help desk has just confirmed that you do have one of our vending machines and someone has requested we come and repair it earlier this afternoon.'

'No. We don't have one.'

'Well in that case there's not much more I can do. I'll just have to leave it. Goodbye.'

'Alright. But when are you going to send someone to repair our coffee machine?'

'I don't understand. What do you mean?'

'I called your company to report our coffee machine not working.'

By now Barney was starting to lose his cool. He didn't know what the hell was this woman talking about.

'I still don't understand. You said you didn't have a vending machine.'

'We don't. Our machine gives free drinks. To be a vending machine it would have to sell drinks. The word vend means to sell. I suggest you look it up.'

He wasn't usually lost for words, but he didn't have a response to this one. He didn't even know whether she was literally correct or not. He was led to the machine and remedied the problem.

Driving home he was feeling a bit bewildered. Did that woman really need to be so stubborn and difficult? He had behaved with impeccable manners and was trying to help her. But there was no way he could keep up false niceties when faced with people such as this, no matter how many written warnings came his way.

6

He'd had a much better sleep than the previous night, and it was another warm, sunny morning, so he repeated the bacon sandwich, mug of tea, and newspaper trick. But halfway through his leisurely breakfast he was rudely interrupted. His phone flashed up 'Sweary'. Barney thought it was unusually early in the morning for her to be calling him. Usually when she phoned, it was to send him somewhere urgently. And indeed it was.

'I've sent you a call for Windsor Racecourse. They've got a coffee machine that isn't working and they are desperate for it to be fixed today. They were really good about it too, so I promised them you'd be there as soon as possible. Is there any chance you could make it your next call?'

'Of course I can. You know me. I'll do anything to help anyone'

'You don't need to give me that load of old pony. But thanks. Will you let me know when you've fixed it?'

He assured her he would and as soon as he'd finished his breakfast and the crossword, he set off for Windsor Racecourse, which was only four miles from the cafe, so he arrived in less than ten minutes. The racecourse looked splendid in the morning sun and he took the opportunity to have a little stroll alongside the deserted and silent track before reporting for duty. These little escapes were essential for his wellbeing. To him they were a type of meditation. They kept him sane. Or rather kept him less insane.

Out of Order

He'd been to this machine before. It was in one of the bars, and it stood there doing nothing for weeks on end, then on a race day got absolutely hammered nonstop for six hours. This was the sort of job he dreaded. There was extra pressure. The staff there treated him with respect, and he so desperately wanted to get their machine working. He would feel terrible if he had to tell them it couldn't be repaired, or it needed a part which he didn't have with him on the day.

The site contact was a man called Graham, who Barney had met on his previous visits. He was usually a calm and amicable man, but today he came across as a little bit on edge.

'Please get it working, if you can. We've got racing this evening and this machine sells literally hundreds of coffees during a race meeting.'

'No problem. Let' s have a look at it.'

Graham left him to it and wandered off as he said he had a lot to do.

Barney got to work. It didn't take him long to diagnose the fault. It was a pump not working, which was good news in that it was fairly easy to change. The big question was whether or not he had a spare one in his car.

On the way to the car his phone went off again. Yet again it said 'Sweary'.

'Yes Mary. What can I do for you this time?'

'I was just wondering how you got on at Windsor Racecourse. Richard is asking.'

'Give me a break Mary! Do you think I'm superman or something? I'm on site now. I told you I'd let you know when I'm done.'

'Right. Thanks.' She detected some irritation in his tone and let him go.

Barney walked to his car and rummaged through his boxes of parts. Much to his relief he found a new pump. From then on it was plain sailing. He fitted the new pump, allowed the machine to heat up, and tested all the different varieties of coffees and chocolates. Then he went to find Graham to give him the good news.

Graham was delighted.

'Thank you so much. You're a hero. It wouldn't matter so much normally, but with it being a race evening it was crucial.'

Barney said, 'No problem. Glad I could help. I didn't even know there was such a thing as evening racing.'

'Oh yes. We have regular evening meetings throughout the summer. The racing is usually followed by a music concert. Tonight, we've got a Queen tribute band.'

'That sounds great.'

'I'll give you a pair of tickets if you want?'

'Oh. Thanks very much. That's brilliant.'

Graham popped into his office and came back with two tickets. They had VIP stamped on them. He wasn't sure what that meant, but it looked good. Graham explained they would get him and his guest into the VIP lounge and enclosure, but they would need to read the conditions, including a dress code, on the back. Barney thanked him again and went back to his car to phone Mary. How he wished all of his customers were like that. Graham wasn't daft either. If Barney was given a pile of work to do and had to choose which site to go to first, would he go to the one where they treat him with contempt and ridicule, or would he go to the one where they give him free race tickets? Graham knows he would get priority treatment, and deservedly so.

Barney's main concern now was that the machine didn't pack up again halfway through the evening. Of course, it was unlikely the new pump would pack up, but there were plenty of other things that could go wrong with it. He would feel so bad if the machine didn't last the evening.

His other concern was that he had nobody to go to the races with. He could ask his dad if he wanted to go. But that wouldn't be much fun. He wasn't into horse racing anyway. He could try Liam, but didn't know if he was interested in horse racing either. He knew he was a motor racing fanatic, but horses didn't have engines. He had karate classes in the evening, but he'd give him a call anyway. He might prefer a night out at the gee-gees and have a few drinks instead of being thrown around.

He had to call Mary first, and took the opportunity to wind her up. It would be his revenge for her harassment earlier.

She answered. 'Hello Barney. I hope you're calling me to tell me all is well at Windsor Racecourse.

'I'm afraid not, I couldn't fix the machine. I don't know what's wrong with it. I tried my best.'

'Oh shit. Richard's going to go mad. What are we going to do? Shall I send another engineer to have a try?'

Barney enjoyed listening to her getting flustered for a while before putting her out of her misery.

'No. I'm only winding you up. Obviously, I've fixed it. I'm a genius. You should know that by now.'

'You knobhead!'

'Sorry, I didn't quite catch that, Mary. Did you say, "Well done Barney, you're amazing"?'

'No, I fucking didn't.'

'Thanks for your appreciation.'

'Were they grateful?'

'Well, a damned sight more grateful than you are. They gave me two free tickets for tonight's racing.'

'Oh, you lucky thing. I love horse racing. Couldn't you get one for me?'

Barney paused. Could he withstand a whole evening with Mary? It would be a shame to waste the ticket. And she sounded really keen. His softer side took over.

'You can have this ticket. I won't be able to find anyone else to go at such short notice.'

He hoped that hadn't sounded insulting. But he needn't have worried.

'Yes! Get in! I can't wait. Thanks so much.'

Out of Order

He thought her reaction was a bit over the top. Did she really love horse racing? Or did she just not get out much? He suspected not. And he was right. Mary didn't have much of a social life. She came across as a larger-than-life character, but was in reality quite lonely.

They both lived a short enough taxi ride to Windsor, but from different directions.

Barney told her, 'I'll meet you outside the main gate at seven o'clock.'

'Brilliant. I haven't been on a date for ages.'

'Wait. No. Mary. I didn't mean it's a date. I...'

But the line was dead. She'd gone before she could have heard that last half sentence. He had to call her back because he forgot to tell her about the dress code for the VIP lounge. But he didn't have the courage to bring up her comment about it being a date.

This wasn't something he had been expecting to do this evening. A free night out at the racing, with a woman he never knew socially, who thought she was going on a date. Oh well. It should make for an entertaining evening.

They met outside the main entrance as agreed exactly on time. They walked to the gate to show their tickets, but one of the staff on the gate stopped them. 'No sir, this is not your entrance. You need the VIP entrance just along there.'

He pointed to where they should go and they found the correct way in. Barney felt uncomfortable being a VIP. Mary loved it.

The VIP area dress code was basically no jeans or trainers, and a shirt with a collar. Barney usually wore a t-shirt and jeans. His only shirts with collars he had were his work ones, but he wasn't going to turn up with Vendetta-Refreshingly Simple on his chest. Luckily, he managed to find a proper shirt hanging somewhere towards the back of his wardrobe. When Mary appeared, she looked like she'd had a lot more experience at dressing smartly. She was wearing an expensive looking blue dress that wouldn't have looked out of place on ladies day at Royal Ascot. Thankfully she hadn't bothered with a hat. He thought she didn't look too bad at all. But it still wasn't going to be a date.

They showed their passes and went to the first bar they came across for a drink.

Mary was impressed.

'This is very nice.'

'So, you're into horse racing then?' he asked.

'Yes. I like a little flutter now and again.'

'In that case we'd better stick a few bets on.'

They had already missed the first race, then had a burger and chips and more drinks while they watched the second race on a screen in the bar. Then they went out to find somewhere to place their bets.

Mary looked at the choices for the third race.

'Ooh look! There's one called Magnificent Mary! I've got to go for that one.'

Barney disagreed. 'But it's 12-1. It's got no chance.'

'What do you know? I won over a hundred quid backing a 16-1 winner in the Grand National last year.'

'That's different. The Grand National has thirty big fences in a race more than four miles long. A lot of the best horses don't even make it to the finish. There is a much better chance for the outsiders to do well. The ones here are just short races with no fences.'

Mary wasn't going to take any notice of him. 'Well, I don't care what you say. I'm putting a fiver on Magnificent Mary to win.'

'Fair enough. It's your own money you're wasting.'

Barney put £2.50 each way on the 2-1 favourite.

They went to the trackside and got an excellent view from the VIP enclosure. An excellent view of Magnificent Mary romping home while the favourite trudged in fourth. Mary was ecstatic.

'Yeeeesss. Get the fuck in!' She screeched in Barney's face while waving her arms in the air, drawing a lot of attention from the other VIPs.

Mary used all her luck up on that one and won nothing else all evening, but ended up well ahead after pocketing the sixty quid. He was beginning to doubt that she was as much of a horse racing expert that she claimed to be. Barney just about broke even using cautious each way bets on favourites.

When the racing was over, they watched I Want To Fake Free,

the Queen tribute band, who were rather good, but neither of them were big Queen fans. A few years ago, the Kaiser Chiefs (the real ones) played a gig here. That would have been much more to Barney's taste. Two weeks ago, it was Elvis (not the real one) providing the entertainment after the racing. Mary would have much preferred that. But it sounded OK, and it was a pleasantly warm evening with a party atmosphere, so they had a few more drinks and stayed until the end.

When it was all over, they headed for the exit, but not before they took a sneaky peek at the coffee machine to make sure it was still working. Much to their relief it was.

Mary said, 'Thanks for the great evening. We must do it again sometime.'

Barney nodded in agreement, but didn't mean it. By this point they both knew neither of them had any romantic feelings for each other.

7

The role of the operator was somewhat different to that of the engineer. They had a routine planned out for them. They would go to the same places at the same times on the same days every week. This suited Alison just fine. She'd seen Barney get stressed out when he was sent to do a horrible job or deal with some dickhead who was having a strop because his bag of crisps was stuck. If anyone started giving her a hard time because their coffee machine wasn't working properly, all she had to do was tell them she would book a call for an engineer to come.

But even though it wasn't her job to do repairs, she would do some of the easier ones anyway. She secretly carried a screwdriver and spanner in her bag. She had become quite proficient solving technical problems at home since her divorce two years ago.

Since her divorce she had learnt to do a lot of things. Her ex-husband had been controlling and belittled her constantly. He would regularly tell her she was fat and ugly. He only allowed her to have a job so she could bring home some money. She couldn't spend any of it on herself. It was a miserable period of her life which she had put up with for far too long.

She had lost touch with all her friends, and was rarely allowed to see her parents, who had both died just before her divorce. Their deaths sparked off a reaction from her, where she'd decided she'd had enough and it was time to fight back.

The only people she ever spoke with were work colleagues, and most of the conversations were about vending machines and the company management. She felt she had also missed out on the chance to have children. Her ex-husband didn't want any, and he made the decisions.

Since finding the strength to leave him she now had a new sense of freedom. She realised she had never been ugly, but could do with losing a bit of weight. So, she joined a gym soon after her divorce and two years of hard work had paid off. A more difficult challenge was giving up her forty cigarettes a day. It was going OK though. It had now been five weeks since her last one.

Although it wasn't her responsibility to remedy faults, customers would often moan at her if something wasn't perfect, and she came up against her fair share of the crackpots that Barney was always moaning about. In fact, she was about to encounter one right now.

Her first job today was in Staines filling a snack machine with various chocolate bars and crisps, and emptying the cash box. But she was interrupted by a man who wanted to point something out to her.

'Can you do something about the screen on this machine?'

'Such as?'

'We can't read what it says. The machine used to be on the other side of the room, but we moved it near the window. Now whenever the sun is shining, we can't read the screen.'

Out of Order

Alison pondered what would be the best way to respond to this. She had always been a strong character who didn't suffer fools gladly. Her terrible marriage had knocked the stuffing out of her. She had become weak and let people walk all over her, and there was no shortage of people who were willing to do that. But she was on the way back up. She was getting stronger. She wasn't going to take any crap from anyone anymore.

Today she kept a cool head and did what she was supposed to do. She rang the helpdesk and explained the situation to Mary, who was as subtle as ever.

'Well, what the fuck do they expect you to do about it? Tell the stupid bastards to move the machine back to where it was, or buy some fucking blinds. We can't move the sun, or rotate the fucking building. How often does the sun shine in Staines anyway? Morons.'

Alison thanked Mary then turned to the man and gave a cleaned-up version of her advice.

'I've just consulted with our help desk. They say there's nothing much we can do. They suggest putting the machine back where it used to be or get some blinds. Do you get many sunny days around these parts?'

He wasn't very happy about it, but she'd done her bit and was glad to get out of there.

She phoned Barney. After all he was the engineer responsible for this machine. But she had no doubt he would have treated them with derision. She knew he would enjoy hearing about it, and he did. They had a good laugh about it. But he also told her there was a way to increase the brightness of the screen in the program, and it only took a minute to do. Not that he was going to hurry to do it. He just told her to forget about it for now, and book an engineer job on the morning of his next darts match, so he could have a quick and easy call up his sleeve when he needed to get away early.

The rest of Alison's day was uneventful. She had hurried to finish her route faster than usual because she had an eye test at the opticians in the afternoon. Not that there was anything wrong with her eyesight. A leaflet had come through her letterbox inviting her for an eye test, and she wanted to take up the offer. She was determined to take care of herself now that she had the freedom to do so.

Hurrying through her work had paid off much better than she had expected. She had got to the shopping centre in High Wycombe with an hour to spare, so took the opportunity to do a bit of shopping. She treated herself to some new gear for the gym, and bought a new pair of jeans, which were a size smaller around the waist than the previous ones she bought.

She was feeling quite happy, although the craving for a cigarette was strong, she was determined to be stronger. Then she arrived at the opticians.

She hadn't been for an eye test for many years. The tests were a lot more complicated than she expected. She assumed there would be just a chart with letters for her to read, starting with big letters at the top and getting smaller towards the bottom. Just like in cartoons. But there was much more to it than that.

They had a whole range of fancy equipment and tests. They even blew a puff of air into her eyes at one stage. One of the tests was for peripheral vision, which involved putting her head inside a box and pressing a button when she saw little stars. Just like playing a computer game. She was made to repeat this test three times, which was slightly concerning. The girl carrying out the tests then disappeared for a while to speak to one of her colleagues, which was even more worrying. When she returned, she said they would like to repeat the pressure test.

They completed everything they wanted to do, and asked Alison to wait in the reception. After ten long minutes a senior looking man approached her. He handed her a piece of paper.

'I'm afraid your tests have shown unusually high pressure readings in your eyes. You need to call this number and book an appointment to go to this hospital as soon as possible.'

Alison felt numb. She trudged back to her van with the piece of paper in her hand. This didn't sound good. Why hadn't they given her a better explanation? Or a bit of reassurance? Of course, it's their job and they do it all day, every day, but they are diagnosing people's eyes, not coffee machines.

She drove home in a hurry and fired up her laptop, hoping for some internet medical advice that would ease her worries. But she didn't find any. All she found were things that would make her feel worse.

8

Vendetta had a department called logistics. Their chief task was moving machines around. Delivering new machines to customers. Collecting old machines that were at the end of their useful life. Collecting machines from customers who had just lost patience with Vendetta and were switching to a different supplier.

The logistic team worked in pairs mostly. This made it easy for the rest of the staff to give them nicknames. They were mainly unflattering, and maybe not always deserved. There were double acts such as Cannon and Ball, The Chuckle Brothers, Little and Large, and Dumb and Dumber. It wasn't as if they weren't good at what they did. It was just that when an engineer had to accompany them on a job, something usually went wrong.

Barney had to do such a job today. The pair he had to accompany him were known as Laurel and Hardy. The task he was faced with was to decommission a canned drink machine and a snack machine which were situated in the foyer of a hotel near Heathrow airport, which Laurel and Hardy would take away. He didn't anticipate any problems.

On arrival at the hotel car park, he saw what he assumed was Laurel and Hardy's lorry. Hardy jumped out and introduced himself. Hardy was the boss and Laurel was the driver.

'Are you the Vendetta engineer?'

Out of Order

'Yes, I am,' said Barney, hoping that the man's inability to read the company logo on his shirt wasn't a sign of things to come.

Hardy continued, 'Did you get the special instructions for this job?'

'No,' said Barney, 'as usual they haven't told me anything. What sort of special instructions?'

Hardy took out a piece of paper. On it were the special instructions. He read them out. 'You must not speak to the hotel staff or let them know what you are doing. Don't let them see you removing the machines.'

Barney had never been given such an odd instruction. He thought he'd better check with Mary. He called her.

'Hello Mary. Laurel and Hardy have just told me we've got to remove two vending machines from a hotel without them seeing us doing it. Is that correct?'

'Yes. It is.'

'Are you for real?'

'Don't blame me. It wasn't my idea. I'm just the messenger.'

'How the hell are we going to get two huge vending machines past the hotel reception without them noticing?'

'That's your problem mate.'

'It shouldn't be. I'm an engineer, not a professional burglar. Is it even legal?'

'I doubt it.'

'Have you gone mad? I don't think it will be possible.'

'Oh, come on. There must be a way. You could turn on your charm with the receptionist. Ask her out. Only don't take her to the races. That's our special thing. While she's distracted, they can sneak past with the machines.'

'Oh right! Brilliant! She's going to be so excited to be going on a date with me that she won't be able to spot two enormous vending machines getting wheeled past her?'

They argued about it for a few minutes, but nothing he said was going to change her mind. So, he told Hardy they were going ahead.

Barney walked into the reception area and came face to face with the receptionist. A man. So, Mary's plan was a non-runner straight away. Not that he was going to do it anyway. The man said, 'Can I help you sir?'

This raised another problem Barney hadn't thought of. He was so busy thinking how he was going to get the machines out that he forgot about getting in unnoticed. All he could think of saying was a feeble, 'I'm working on the vending machine.' Which was true enough. He carried out the decommissioning of the machines as quickly as he could, then Laurel and Hardy loaded one onto a pump truck. They sheepishly wheeled it past the reception desk, and the man on the reception desk said, 'Oh. You're taking it outside then?'

'Er… I don't know,' replied Hardy, not having a clue what else to say.

They loaded the machine onto the lorry and returned for the other one.

Out of Order

Barney was relieved that it was all going fairly well. If they could just get the other machine on the lorry without any further questions being asked, they might just get away with it. He should have known better.

A bunch of irate hotel guests came through the front door and started yelling at the receptionist. They were complaining that some idiot had parked a lorry in front of the airport shuttle bus, preventing it from driving off, and they were worried that they were going to miss their flights. That idiot was Laurel.

Barney told him, 'You'd better move the lorry. We don't want to draw attention to ourselves.'

Laurel went out to move it, but was gone a worryingly long time. Meanwhile the angry mob demanded to speak with the manager. The receptionist called the manager, who appeared shortly. But the manager's immediate concern wasn't for his guests.

'Where the hell are you going with my vending machine?' he shouted.

Before anyone could come up with an answer, Laurel returned. 'I can't find the lorry keys.'

That was enough for Barney. He told them he had to go to his car. Which he did. And he got in. And he drove away as fast as he could.

Barney didn't know what was going to happen next, but he didn't really care. He was just glad to be out of there. He was expecting to be getting a phone call from Bowles. And he did, just over an hour after he had done a runner.

'Cecil. What on earth is going on? Logistics say you abandoned them and left them in a difficult situation.'

Barney decided attack was the best form of defence. 'A situation of their own making. They are a pair of clowns. If they hadn't blocked the airport shuttle bus, and if they hadn't lost their keys, there wouldn't have been any problem.'

'You should have stayed with them.'

'Why? I'd done the decommissioning. That's all I was there for. Next time you want some vending machines stealing, send someone else.'

'We weren't stealing them. They belong to us. They refused to pay their bill.'

'Well maybe that should have been negotiated in advance. Just out of curiosity, how did it all end up?'

'The hotel blocked our lorry in with a vehicle of their own and wouldn't let it go until we unloaded the vending machine. Which we did. They also want us to pay the bill for taxis they hired to get their guests to the airport.'

'So now they've got two vending machines that don't work.'

'Yes. You may have to go back to recommission them. If they pay the bill.'

'Terrific,' said Barney. 'Did Laurel ever find his lorry keys?'

'Laurel?'

'Never mind.'

'Yes. They were in his pocket.'

9

Barney had first become friends with Alison two years ago on a work beano to Brighton. When he first heard about the outing, he thought it would be good fun, having a day at the seaside and a few beers, hopefully get to know a few people a bit better, and meet some people he'd never met before. He had the view that it was a good idea to have as many allies as possible among the workers. There were no managers on the trip. It wasn't an official Vendetta function. It had been arranged by the staff at the Winchester office.

The coach was starting off in High Wycombe, with pick up points at Reading, Basingstoke and Winchester. Barney joined the coach at Reading.

Once the coach was full, he realised he didn't know very many of the people who were going. Liam had only been working there for a short while and didn't come on the trip. Mary didn't join the company until just before Christmas later that year. Alison was there, but he was surprised to see her. Their paths had crossed at work because they were covering the same area, but they hadn't got to know each other. She was quiet and shy. She wasn't with anyone particular on the trip and looked like she wasn't good at making friends. Apart from a few of the office staff who worked in the same building, most of the people on the coach did jobs out on the road, so most of them didn't know each other very well.

On the journey down, Barney was sitting next to someone he'd never met. He was one the office staff, called Andy. Andy was friendly and talkative, and Barney chatted to him at first, but gradually began to find him hard work. Before long he realised the bloke was a complete and utter twat. He would have been far happier to be left alone, relaxing and looking out of the window, watching the fields go by. It got worse when they arrived in Brighton and were driving through the town. Andy had to comment on every female they drove past.

'Look at the size of those. She'll have someone's eye out! Phwarr. Look at her. I would. Would you?'

'Of course you would, you pathetic little man, but you wouldn't be able to because no woman in her right mind would touch you with a barge pole', thought Barney, wanting to shout it out at the top of his voice so the rest of the coach could hear, but resisting the temptation for the sake of not causing a scene.

It continued until the coach parked.

'Eeuurgh! Look at that one. She's got a face like a sack of spanners.'

Barney couldn't wait to get out of the coach. He had been looking forward to today, and liked having a drink as much as anybody. But he was strangely not in the mood for partying. Hopefully he would snap out of it when he could get away from Andy and start to enjoy himself.

The coach parked close to the pier, and everyone piled into the nearest pub. It was a beautiful sunny day, and the twinkling sea was flat. He liked being by the sea. He found it therapeutic. But he doubted there would be much in the way of outdoor activity today.

After two or three drinks, the group were getting louder, and restless. They all moved en masse to a large bar on the pier which had a karaoke going on. It was noisy, and full of people similar to the Vendetta crowd, on work outings, or on holiday.

They were still in there two hours later, and Barney doubted they would be leaving until it was time to get back on the coach. He wasn't keen on karaoke. Most of the singing was awful, and he couldn't sing either, but at least he knew it, and wouldn't inflict it on others. Therefore, he was horrified when one of the others asked him what he was going to sing.

'No, no. I'm not doing one. I'm happy to just sit here and watch.'

'Oh yes you are. We all have to. If you don't pick a song, I'll choose one for you.'

Twenty minutes later he'd had enough and decided to sneak out and go somewhere else. Just as he reached the door, the girl in charge of the karaoke announced, 'and next up is Barney, who is going to sing Rock and Roll by Led Zeppelin.'

He quietly slipped out of the door unnoticed.

Much to his delight, he found another bar further along the promenade that had a TV with the cricket on. England were playing India. He bought a pint and settled there. This was much more to his liking. Sitting in a bar with a pleasant view overlooking the sea, and cricket to watch. And no karaoke. Led Zeppelin? What were they thinking? He didn't even know the song. He watched the cricket until they went off for the tea break.

Then he went for a walk along the promenade. He was enjoying himself now. The rest of them were happy in the karaoke bar, and he was happy not being in the karaoke bar.

While he was wandering, he saw Alison sitting alone staring out to sea. He wasn't sure if he should disturb her. He looked from a distance for a while, but the beer had reduced his inhibitions and he walked up to her.

He asked her, 'Hello. Do you mind if I join you?'

She replied, 'No, not at all.'

'What are you doing sitting out here?'

'I had to escape from the karaoke. It's not my idea of fun. I don't mind singing, but not in public.'

'Same here. They were going to make me sing a Led Zeppelin song. I managed to sneak out in the nick of time.'

She gave half a laugh.

'They had me down to sing Gloria Gaynor's I will survive. I don't know if that was someone's idea of a joke. I'm going through a divorce at the moment.'

'Oh. I'm sorry to hear that.'

'Don't be. It's something I should have done a long time ago. It's the reason I came on this trip. I thought it was time to make the most of my new freedom. I wouldn't have been allowed to come on anything like this when I was married. But it was a mistake coming here. I'm not enjoying it at all.'

'Me neither,' said Barney. 'I intend to spend the rest of the day watching cricket in that little bar along the promenade. You can join me if you want?'

'No thanks. Cricket is even worse than Karaoke. Oh sorry. I didn't mean to be rude.'

'No problem. I've heard a lot worse.'

'I'm just going to do a bit of shopping instead.'

'Alright. I'll see you on the coach then.'

'I didn't think much of your friend on the coach. He was making the most horrible sexist comments.'

'I know. And he's not my friend. I'd never met him before until this morning. I thought he was horrible too. In fact, I don't want to sit next to him on the return journey.'

'You can sit with me instead if you want?'

'Yes. That would be good, if you don't mind.'

Alison went shopping and Barney returned to the bar with the cricket.

The return journey was tough to endure. The volume of the shouting, laughing, and singing was horrendous. and there was a strong smell of fish and chips. Barney and Alison sat together and tried to keep a low profile. Andy hadn't noticed that Barney wasn't sitting next to him any longer.

Barney got out at Reading. By then the coach was half empty, and quieter. Alison stayed on until the final destination at High Wycombe.

Barney had a short train journey from Reading to get home. During the journey he looked up Rock and Roll by Led Zeppelin on his phone, then played it very loud through his earphones. He was surprised to find that he liked it. But he was happy that he hadn't tried to sing it and made a fool of himself.

10

Barney was carrying a passenger today. Liam worked in the adjacent patch to him, although they often crossed over the border to help each other out. He was the only real friend Barney had at work. They didn't have a great lot in common, but it was a useful alliance. Barney was the better engineer. Older, wiser, and more experienced. Liam often relied on him for advice, or to go along on a job with him to get him out of trouble.

In return, Liam was younger, stronger, eager to please, and was useful when Barney needed to move a machine or needed something heavy lifting. They also would go to the pub for a pint when work was getting them down. Or even when it wasn't.

Occasionally they would go out on a Saturday evening to a few pubs, followed by a visit to Liam's favourite club, where there was music, dancing, and lots of girls. It wasn't Barneys scene. He didn't like dance music. Or dancing. He preferred electric guitars. But he went along because Liam always managed to attract girls. It was an arrangement that worked for Liam too. Having Barney along as his wingman meant he always got the good looking one, while Barney had to take his chances with her mate.

Today they had to work together because Liam was temporarily without a car. His car had gone in for a service and there had been a typical Vendetta cockup getting him a replacement vehicle. So, Mary suggested rather than sit around doing nothing, he hung out with Barney for the day.

'You might fucking learn something you dickhead,' is how she tried to suggest the idea to him.

'Oh, don't worry about Mary. That's just her way of telling you how much she likes you,' Barney reassured him.

Barney picked him up at his house in Beaconsfield and took him to his favourite cafe. Liam wasn't impressed.

'Do you have a bacon sandwich every morning?' he asked.

'No. Sometimes I go for the full English breakfast.'

Liam was a lot more health conscious than Barney. He kept himself fit by going jogging and swimming. Also, he did regular karate classes.

'It's not good for your health eating fatty fry ups every day.'

'It makes me happy. And being happy is good for your health.'

'You're out of shape.'

'I'm fine thanks.'

They finished their breakfast and drove to their first call, which was in Slough Trading Estate, a place where a lot of Barney's customers were.

He told Liam, 'I bet you didn't know Thunderbirds was invented in Slough Trading Estate?'

'What's a thunder bird?'

'You've never heard of Thunderbirds?'

'No.'

'I used to watch it on telly when I was a kid. It had puppets and strange aircraft and stuff. They were called International Rescue. They used to save people who were in danger, operating from a secret island.'

'How can you keep an island secret?'

'I don't know. But they managed to.'

'Why did they even need to be a secret? The fire brigade doesn't keep itself hidden. They have easy to be found fire stations with 'Fire Brigade' in big letters on the front.'

'OK, I concede it wasn't true to life. In fact, in one scene Lady Penelope was in her Rolls Royce on the M1 and it was the only car on the road. When has the M1 ever been like that? I think she might have been driving on the wrong side of the road too. But I was just a kid, so I didn't care about reality. I'm surprised you haven't heard of it though. It was very famous.'

'I probably wasn't even born.'

'I suppose you've never heard of Stingray or Captain Scarlet either?'

'Nah. To be honest, they sound a bit naff.'

'How dare you! Heretic. We'll be driving past the place they were made in a minute. I was going to show you where it was, but there's not much point now. You've ruined the moment.'

They arrived at their destination. It looked like a fairly routine job. Machine not accepting coins.

This particular customer was what they called a DIY site. In other words, the customer did all the cleaning and filling themselves, and they collected the money. Vendetta just dealt with technical problems.

There was a woman who dealt with this machine and she took them to it.

Barney's initial investigation found that the coin controller, a fragile collection of electronics in a flimsy plastic case, no doubt costing a few hundred quid, was completely dead. After watching him poke around with it for 20 minutes, she said, 'If it helps, there was a coin stuck, so I took it out and gave it a good shaking. That didn't work so I bashed it a few times until the coin fell out. I don't understand why it is dead.'

'Well, I may be wrong, but I've just got this hunch why it might not be working. Just a sneaking suspicion.'

He had no idea if she understood what he was inferring.

He went to the car and brought a new coin controller, which he fitted and tested. He explained to the woman what he'd done.

'I've fitted a brand new, expensive, delicate, fragile coin controller. Your machine is now working just fine.'

She thanked them, then wandered off to do something else. They sat down and had a coffee.

'She's probably off to demolish another part of the building.' suggested Barney.

'You don't give anyone the benefit of the doubt, do you? I mean, she's clearly as mad as a box of frogs.' replied Liam.

'I thought I went fairly easy on her. I can't afford not to with

Bowles breathing down my neck. Anyway, it hacks me off when these amateurs think they can fix things by bashing the hell out of them.'

'I suppose you've got a point. I just would have given her a bit more leeway than you did, that's all.'

'That's probably because you fancy her. And I gave her quite a bit of leeway. I could have sent her an invoice for that. The service contract doesn't cover acts of vandalism.'

'I don't fancy her.'

'Come off it. You fancy every female as long as she's got a pulse.'

They finished their coffees and went outside. Liam said, 'Do you feel like having a pint after work?'

'No. I feel like having a pint during work. It tastes much better that way.' replied Barney.

'I can't have too many. I've got my karate class this evening.'

'If I did karate, I'd need to have a few pints beforehand to get me through it.'

'I'm not surprised. Look at the state of you.'

'What do you mean? There's nothing wrong with me.'

'Too much booze. You could do with some exercise too. Take up a sport.'

'I play darts, don't I?'

'Oh yes, that's very healthy. Walk back and forward for five minutes while downing half a dozen pints.'

Liam had a point. But he was younger and stronger. He had reached a decent standard in his karate. A useful friend to have around if ever he gets threatened. Barney used to play football and cricket. He wasn't a bad player at both. But he was 45 now. He couldn't keep playing forever.

Their last call was in the centre of Windsor and afterwards they had two pints each in a pub next to the castle.

Liam again brought up the subject of difficult customers.

Barney told him, 'You're still relatively new to this job. You'll meet your share eventually. Someone who'll treat you with utter contempt.'

Liam asked, 'Why do you think so many people act like that?'

'I blame Red Dwarf.'

'What the hell are you on about?'

'Wait a minute. Don't tell me you've never heard of Red Dwarf either? It's a comedy on the telly with four smegheads flying a spaceship three million years in the future. I suppose you think that sounds naff too?'

'I know what Red Dwarf is. I'm a big fan. I just don't see what it's got to do with what we were talking about.'

'There's a character none of the others like. They treat him with ridicule and contempt. It gets mentioned several times throughout the series that his main duty was servicing the ship's vending machine. Every time it crops up it is accompanied by raucous laughter. They are implying that only the biggest idiot would have the job of looking after the vending machine. So, people who watch it treat us accordingly. Do you see what I mean?'

'I think you're losing the plot mate,' said Liam.

Barney was getting agitated. He would usually be the one who was winding Liam up. But today it was happening the other way around. And Liam could tell. He was enjoying it.

'I think it's just you. I went on a skiing holiday in February and there were loads of posh girls there. There were also plenty of bullshitters trying to convince the girls they were surgeons, stockbrokers, and professional tennis players. But when I told them I repaired vending machines, I got far more attention from the women than the other blokes.'

Barney wasn't convinced. 'That's never happened to me.'

'Like I said. I think it's just you. I think you ought to be nicer to people.'

'I am nice to people. I only get pissed off with them when they do something to piss me off.'

'Come off it. This morning you blasted your horn at that poor girl. She jumped out of her skin.'

'Ah, you mean the poor girl who, despite there being a perfectly good footpath, was walking on the road with her back to the traffic wearing headphones?'

'Yes.'

'I was doing her a favour. I could even have saved her life, because next time she might realise what a stupid thing it was to do, and not do it.'

'You might have a point on that one. But what about last week when we were at the supermarket checkout? You were so rude to that old lady who was rummaging through her handbag trying to find her purse.'

'That was because she'd been standing in the queue for ten minutes, and only started looking for it when she had to pay. How can anyone not get frustrated at that?'

Barney changed the subject. They talked about the Christmas party that the company had just announced. It was going to be held in some place in London Docklands. The company were even going to lay on a fleet of minibuses to get people home afterwards.

'Yes, I'm looking forward to it,' said Barney. 'Free food and drink if nothing else.'

Liam had different priorities. 'And what about all those women, getting drunk and losing their inhibitions?'

Barney tutted, and shook his head. 'See what I mean? Anything with a pulse! Have you seen any of the girls in the office that you may be interested in?'

'Well yes, I have as a matter of fact. There's someone I really like.'

'And who might that be?'

'I'm not telling you. You'd only laugh. What about you? Do you have anyone in mind?'

'No. as you know, I don't have much luck with women.'

11

It was two days after Alison's visit to the opticians. It was dull and blustery. Barney went to the cafe again and had a bacon sandwich. He wasn't going to allow a few snide remarks from Liam to deprive him of one of life's great pleasures. He enjoyed his sandwich and mug of tea as much as ever and read all the back pages of the newspaper. He didn't usually bother with the front pages. They were full of mindless showbiz gossip, royal family stuff, or politicians spouting garbage. Then he drove to his first call of the day.

He was sent to a computer manufacturer in Slough. It was another new contract, so it was his first visit there. On arrival he spotted Alison's van in the car park. Hopefully he would catch her before she left. They could have a coffee and put the world to right. Or at least put the company to right. In general, they had the same opinions about the same people, so it made for easy conversation. It was almost therapeutic, pointing out faults of people you didn't like to someone who agreed with you.

As he usually did before he turned up at a customer's reception, Barney had read all the information on his screen he'd been sent about the job. Quite often a lot of important points were missing, such as machine location, or description of fault. But it was always better to arrive as well prepared as possible.

Everything looked straightforward. Or rather it was until he noticed the site contact name. It was Wan Ki. This provoked a childish snigger from Barney, which continued until he arrived at the revolving door indicating the reception.

Then an awful thought occurred to him. There was a good chance the receptionist would ask him if he knew who she needed to call. How would he keep a straight face? Was he about to embarrass himself? Perhaps she wouldn't ask. Maybe she already knew which one of her colleagues dealt with vending machine issues and would just call him.

He approached the reception desk.

'Good morning. How can I help you?'

'Hi. I'm from Vendetta. I'm here to repair your vending machine.'

'Oh good. Have you been given a name to contact?'

Barney tried desperately not to laugh. It was painful.

'Errm. I'll just check.'

He pretended to read his screen.

'Errrm. I err, I can't really make it out without my glasses. I think it says Wan.'

'Oh, that must be Wan Ki. I'll just call him.'

The receptionist made the phone call and turned back to Barney.

'He's just coming.'

Why did she have to say that? Barney turned away from her before she could see his face and hurried out the door shouting that he had to go back to the car for something.

Now that he'd managed to lose his composure once, what

chance did he have of keeping it when Mister Ki appeared. He blamed the receptionist. She could have said, 'He's on his way' instead.

He did appear, and when Barney saw he was about 6 ft 7, any possibilities of laughing evaporated.

Wan Ki took Barney to the machine and then went off to do something else. Alison was busy filling the machine with fresh coffee. She had her back to him.

'Oh Alison. Wait 'til I tell you this. It was so embarrassing… '

She didn't make any sound or even turn around. He stepped alongside her and saw tears streaming down her face. She turned to look at him and broke down completely. She was now sobbing out loud.

Barney wasn't good in these situations. He didn't know how to deal with it. Should he hug her? Should he hand her a tissue? In the end he just settled for 'Do you want to go outside?'

She nodded and followed him out the door and they went to sit in her van.

He asked her 'Would you like to talk about it?'

It was the only thing he could think of saying. He really was quite useless at this. She cried for a little while longer, then managed to compose herself and told him about her visit to the opticians. She had been reading all kinds of horrible things on the Internet, and saw some gruesome pictures.

'I'm so scared' she said, and started crying again.

'Have you called the hospital yet?'

'Yes. But the earliest appointment they can give me is not for another six weeks.'

'Well maybe that's a good sign. If they thought you were in imminent danger of losing your eyesight, they would have got you in straight away'

She didn't say anything.

'Do you have someone to go with you to the hospital?'

'No.'

'I can come along with you if you want?'

She nodded.

'Maybe you should go home'

'No, no. I'll be alright in a minute'

'Well take it easy and try not to worry. Call me anytime if you need to.'

She managed to compose herself enough to go back to the machine to finish replenishing it. Then she drove off in her van while Barney stayed to repair the fault.

He went back to tell Wan Ki (which all of a sudden wasn't funny anymore, if indeed it ever was) that his machine was now working. Then he just sat in his car for a while. He felt terrible for Alison. He'd seen people act like the world was coming to an end because a vending machine hadn't given them their 10p change, but he'd never seen anyone as genuinely upset as that. His own money worries were tiny in comparison.

There was more drama to follow. As he drove out of the car

park his car made contact with a cyclist who was on the footpath, weaving through pedestrians and had gone straight across the car park exit without looking. The reaction of the cyclist was extraordinary. Despite the fact that he was completely in the wrong, and endangering himself and others, he started shouting and swearing, and making obscene gestures with his hand. Barney was in the mood to wrap the bike around his neck. He shouted a few choice words of his own, and angrily climbed out of the car, but the cyclist was heading off into the distance before anything else could happen.

Something else did happen, but was just a minor irritation. His phone rang and displayed the name Colin. Colin was another of the engineers, and often called Barney to talk about nothing in particular. Barney found it impossible to end a phone call with him and often just hung up.

'Hiya Barn. How's it going?'

'Alright.'

'We got cut off last time I was on the phone with you.'

'Yeah. I must have been in a lift or something.'

'I can't remember what we were talking about.'

'Neither can I.'

'So, what's happening?'

'Nothing.'

'So, what are you up too?'

'I'm just contemplating trapping my goolies in a vending machine door,' he mumbled.

'What?'

'Nothing. My battery is really low. I think I'm about to get cut off.'

Barney ended the Call. Colin thought Barney had the worst phone in the world. It cut out every time he was talking to him.

Alison managed to get through the rest of the day. She was trying to convince herself that she was feeling better now that she'd talked to someone, and now that at least she had someone to come to the hospital with her. But her stomach was in knots, and would be that way for the next six weeks.

12

It was the day of another darts match. Barney was hoping for a quiet day without getting hassle from anyone, then he could go along to the pub later and just enjoy himself. That hope was short lived.

His phone rang, and it flashed up 'unknown number'. But Barney knew who it would be.

'Hello.'

'We want £500 by the weekend.'

'I haven't got it. I don't get paid until next week.'

'That's not my problem. Just get it.'

And then he hung up.

Barney couldn't understand how he had ended up in this predicament. It wasn't as if he'd wildly overspent. He'd slowly managed to pay off his overdraft from his university days, but moving away from his parents' house had taken him by surprise. He hadn't realised how many bills had to be paid. Telephone, water, gas, electricity, internet, television licence, credit card, rent, council tax. He didn't even consider these things had to be paid for until he had to move out and live on his own. He wasn't any good at managing his finances. He should have kept an eye on things a bit better. Then he turned to the wrong sort of people for help. He now owed them £7000, which was a lot more than he borrowed from them in the first place. Most the payments he was giving to them were just extortionate interest charges and the debt was never coming down.

It would be an enormous help if he could work at the weekend and get some overtime. Vendetta provided weekend cover for some of its customers, such as hotels, supermarkets, and leisure centres. But to do so he would have to ask Richard Bowles, and following the meeting they had, Bowles was not about to do Barney any favours.

He arrived at a business park which had a barrier and little security hut. Inside was a security guard who stuck his head out of a window and just stared at Barney without speaking. Barney eventually spoke first.

'Good morning. I'm from Vendetta.'

'So, you've come to collect the refuse at last?'

'No. I've come to solve a problem with a vending machine.'

'Oh, you deal with vending machines as well now?'

'Not "as well". Vending machines are the only thing we deal with.'

'So, who's going to take away the refuse?'

'I don't know. Who normally does it?'

'Vendetta'

'No, they don't. I think you're mistaken.'

'I've been working here for 14 years. I know what I'm talking about.'

'I've been working for Vendetta for 12 years. We are a vending machine company. Vending machines are all we deal with.

Nothing else.'

'I'll ring your office and check.'

'They'll tell you the same thing.'

'I'm sure they won't.'

'Well while you're calling them, do you mind if I sort out the vending machine and we'll deal with the other stuff later?'

He reluctantly agreed and raised the barrier.

Encounters such as this drove Barney crazy. The man was clearly wrong, but was far too stubborn to admit it. He would have very much liked to tell him what a prat he was, but under his present circumstances it wouldn't be a sensible move.

The rest of the day dragged slowly by. It was a warm autumn day and Barney was looking forward to a few cold beers. Tonight, they were playing against a team called Johnson & Smith, the dullness of the name reflecting the dullness of their players, who were a lot less friendly than the ones they played last week. But that didn't matter too much. It just meant that the teams didn't mix with each other and talked among themselves.

He managed to catch the train he prefers taking, and it moved along at a reasonable speed, so he got to the pub nice and early. Mickey Mouse Club were back in their home venue, which was a decent pub called the Black Cat, near Moorgate tube station that got packed out for a couple of hours after everyone left their offices, but emptied out in time for them to play their match.

Only Daffy and Tom from the team were in the pub. These two were the least serious about darts in the team. Their priority was drinking and socialising with their friends. Daffy got his nickname when he turned up one evening with a haircut that someone suggested made him look like Daffy Duck. He didn't keep the hairstyle for long, but he has been stuck with the name ever since. The opposition hadn't arrived yet. They normally met somewhere else for a bit of practice and then turned up all at once.

Barney decided not to join in the round this evening. He had to somehow curb his spending. Instead, he bought himself a pint of lager. He was the only lager drinker in the team. The rest of the team were real ale drinkers, apart from Fiona who drank white wine. This meant he had to endure lots of conversations about beer. With lager you just buy it, drink it and never mention it again. The rest of them could waffle away for hours about the choices on offer in the pub. He joined Daffy and Tom, who, he was relieved to discover, were talking about football, so he was able to join in.

By the time the game was due to start, the other three team members had turned up, and as expected the opposition all turned up at all once at the last moment.

The game got underway, and as usual one of the Johnson & Smith team started to moan about a wobbly floorboard on exactly the spot his foot was when he threw. Everyone else threw from the same spot, be he was the only one on both sides who thought there was a wobbly floorboard. From the way he acted anyone would think the home team had deliberately sabotaged the floorboards. Another of them would be moaning later on that the light above the board wasn't bright enough.

Roy had selected Fiona's game to be tonight's lottery leg. Fiona was a very good player, but there was still an outdated, condescending attitude towards female players from some of the men in the darts league. That often worked in her favour. If anyone made any pathetic sexist comments, she had some smart comebacks to make them look small. And If anyone took her ability as a player lightly, she usually murdered them.

Because of her talent she only managed two scores below 60 in her game. Daffy duly obliged with the other four numbers in the following leg, two of which were 26 and 41 as usual. It occurred to the team that if they ever won a prize, 26 and 41 would have to be two of the numbers, and the prize would end up being shared with a hundred other darts teams around the country.

Barney won his singles game in emphatic style and was feeling a lot better than he was at the last match. There was nothing better than hitting a first dart double finish to make you forget your other problems. Of which he had plenty.

Mickey Mouse Club lost the match 6-5 which they weren't overly upset about. By contrast, the winners Johnson & Smith weren't exactly jumping for joy, and it was a relief when they wandered out to return to their own pub, leaving the 'Mice' to enjoy, and talk about the quality of a few more pints.

As closing time approached, Roy checked everybody's availability for the following week. Roy's organisational skills were exceptional. If his darts skills were as good, he'd be playing in the world championship. Barney entertained the idea of employing him as an accountant to run his finances. For free of course. Paying an accountant wouldn't do much towards helping him pay off his debt. Planning as far ahead as the next darts match is about as organised as Barney could get. He confirmed he would be playing next week, because at this stage he thought he would be. But he wouldn't be.

13

On the way to work the next morning there was only one thing on Barney's mind, apart from a bacon sandwich. How was he going to get £500 by tomorrow? Although there wasn't much point in thinking for too long about the answer. He kept coming to the same conclusion. He wasn't going to get £500 by tomorrow. So, what he really should have been thinking about was what the consequences would be when he didn't come up with the money. They weren't nice people. They had threatened him before, but he had always found ways of paying, so he wasn't too sure if they carried out their threats, but figured it would be wise to take them seriously.

Barney's phone rang and 'unknown number' appeared on the screen. It could be them again, but it was unlikely. They had given him until the weekend to pay, therefore he didn't see why would they call now. So he answered.

An official sounding voice said, 'Hello. This is PC Louise Jones from Thames Valley Police. Am I speaking to Cecil Barnard?'

'Yes,' he replied apprehensively.

'I'm calling to inform you we will not be taking any further action.'

'That's great news. But I haven't a clue what you're talking about.'

'About the cyclist who made a complaint against you?'

'No, I never knew anything about any complaint.'

'Well, that's most unusual. You should have been contacted. In that case would you like to give us your versions of events?'

'You might need to narrow it down a bit. I've had quite a few confrontations with cyclists.'

'Have you now?'

Barney immediately wished he hadn't told her that.

PC Louise Jones described the occasion when he was driving out of the car park after visiting Wan Ki.

'Oh. That one. Well, I was driving out of the car park. There was a cyclist on the footpath, weaving through pedestrians at speed, and he suddenly went across the exit in front of me. I was forced to do an emergency stop. There was some contact with my car and his rear wheel, but no damage or injury as far as I could tell. The cyclist shouted something incoherent, I said a few things back, and that was it.'

'What did he shout?'

'I don't know. That's the thing about incoherent.'

'His version of events is a lot different to yours.'

'You don't say. That's not surprising. He was hardly going to say "I'd like to make a complaint about a driver whose quick reactions saved me from being splattered all over the road" is he?'

'He says you threatened to run him over if you saw him again.'

'No, that's not true. What I actually said was "Next time you might not be so lucky". That's a different meaning altogether.'

'So, you deny threatening him?'

'Yes. I never threatened him. He sped off before I had the chance to.'

'Is that an admission that you were going to threaten him?'

'No, I didn't mean it like that. You're twisting my words.'

'What did you mean then?'

'All I was trying to do was point out that he shouldn't be cycling on the pavement. Isn't that something your lot should be doing?'

'Don't try to tell us how to do our job.'

'No. I don't suppose there'd be much point.'

'Anyway, we've decided we will be taking no further action.'

'That's a relief. Or it would have been if I'd known you'd been considering it.'

'Just be more careful in future.'

'Yes, I will. I'll be extremely careful. I'll not leave the house. Ever. I'll just sit at home until I die, shall? While people like him are free to cycle on pavements, ignore red lights, one-way streets and pedestrian crossings, and ride around in the dark without lights. I bet you didn't tell him to be more careful in future?'

But nobody was listening to his rant. PC Louise Jones had long since ended the call.

Barney wondered what the point of it was. Why are so many people making life so difficult for him? But he wasn't allowed much time to wonder for too long.

His phone rang again. The name 'Grumbling Bowels' appeared on the screen. That was just what he needed. He couldn't face a conversation with Richard Bowles right now. So, he just ignored his phone. He would go to his next job, sit down and have a cup of tea and call him back. If he could be bothered.

The job in question was going to be another struggle to not laugh inappropriately. It was a place he'd visited several times before. The receptionist was friendly enough, but she had a voice that sounded like a cartoon mouse, and sometimes it was hard to keep a straight face. On this occasion he had no problems. He wasn't in the mood to laugh at anything today.

While he was doing his work, he received yet another phone call. This time the screen said 'Sweary'. Barney didn't mind that. She usually cheered him up.

'Hi Mary. How can I help you?'

'I just thought that I'd warn you, your mate Richard has been trying to get hold of you.'

'I know. I ignored his call.'

'I think you'd better fucking call him. You're already in his bad books.'

'Don't I know it? Have you any idea what he wants?'

'Yes. Don't worry, it's nothing bad. He just wants to let you know that you're going on a training day next week. There's some new coffee machine coming out and all of the engineers have got to go for a training course to learn about it.'

'OK. Thanks Mary. I'll give him a call.'

Out of Order

Barney finished the job, then got a cup of tea from the machine he'd just got working, and sat down. He would phone Bowles at some point. But he would keep him waiting for a bit longer. He wanted to phone his dad first.

Barney had been named Cecil after his dad. He didn't like the name. He never understood why any parent would want to give their child the same name as them. It only led to lots of confusion in his childhood. It was also quite an old-fashioned name. He'd never come across anyone else called Cecil, especially his age, in his life. So, he was reasonably happy when he moved from Hot Cup to Vendetta and his new workmates started calling him Barney. He never knew any real-life Barneys either. Only fictional ones such as the drunkard in the Simpsons, Fred Flintstone's next-door neighbour, and a big purple dinosaur in a kids programme which he thinks was just called Barney. The singer in the band New Order also had Barney as a nickname, and as they were one of his favourite bands, this added a level of respectability to the name as far as he was concerned. It was also defined in the slang dictionary as 'a noisy quarrel', which some of his workmates thought made it quite appropriate.

Apart from both being called Cecil Barnard, they didn't have much in common. Cricket was the only other thing. They had watched test matches on television together when he was growing up, and his dad had taken him to watch games. These days, arguing about the performances of the England team, or who should and should not be in the team were just about the only conversations they had. His parents had split up when he was 27. His mum was now living in the Lake District running a Bed and Breakfast. He visited her four or five times a year. He found it easy to keep up the regular visits because it was such an attractive part of the world. But for now, he had to get through a conversation with his dad. He hadn't seen him since their trip to the Oval earlier this summer.

'Hello Cecil.'

'Hi dad.'

'How much do you want to borrow this time?'

'I don't want to borrow anything,' he lied. That was the original purpose of the call, but he wasn't going to ask now.

'So why are you calling?'

'Just for a chat.'

'You never ring just for a chat.'

'I am this time.'

'So, you're alright for money then?'

'Yes. Fine.'

'That's good. Because I'm having a few money problems myself.'

That wasn't what Barney was expecting to hear. And it wasn't good news. They talked for a while about his dad's own financial worries, before sorting out the problems of the current England cricket captain, and Barney felt guilty. How he wished he wasn't in this situation and was in a position to help his dad out.

It seemed like he'd been talking on the phone all day. But Barney had one more call to make. He looked up 'Grumbling Bowels' in his contacts and pressed the little green telephone.

Bowles was as charmless as ever. He had booked Barney on a training course learning about a new coffee machine called a Cafeblam 73 which he would soon be required to know how to repair. The training was happening on the following Friday at a hotel in Torquay. Barney found this amusing. Fawlty Towers would be an appropriate venue for a company like Vendetta. He would have to travel there on Thursday afternoon to attend some pointless introductory meeting in the evening.

Unfortunately, this meant he would be missing a darts match. He wouldn't be surprised if Bowles had done that deliberately. Everyone in the office knew Thursday evenings were Barney's darts nights. But he could save a bit of money by not going to a darts match, and an all-expenses paid night in a hotel at the seaside could be a nice break. It would have been better if Liam was coming too. Then they could check out a few pubs. There was always a chance that some of the others on the training course might be interesting company. But it was unlikely. They were usually a tedious bunch.

He wasn't getting much work done today. But he had a very easy job lined up. The customer was a pain. Not the worst he's ever met, just grumpy about everything. But all he had to do was to take off a little plastic pipe which had a crack in it and replace it with a new one. A two-minute job, or so he thought. He should know better than that by now. He checked in with reception and the grumpy man came to meet him. Barney tried in vain to be cheery.

'I've got your replacement pipe.'

'Why's it taken so long?'

''I had to wait for the manufacturers to send me the part. It was out of my control.'

'Hmm. Let's hope it works.'

'It's just a little plastic pipe. Nothing can go wrong.'

As soon as he'd said that, an alarm bell went off in his head. It was as if those very words were a magic spell to make things go wrong.

The parcel containing the part had been delivered this morning and he opened it in front of the grumpy man. He removed the contents. But there was no pipe. Instead, there was a packet of Jelly Babies. Barney held them up and stared at them. Grumpy man also stared at them. Barney searched for something to say.

'Would you like a packet of Jelly Babies?'

'What am I going to do with a packet of Jelly Babies?'

Barney thought long and hard.

'Eat them?'

'I don't like Jelly Babies.'

There was nothing more to be said. He had no explanation to offer. He hadn't got the foggiest idea why he was sent Jelly Babies instead of a part for a coffee machine. It was an embarrassing situation, but clearly not his fault. Sometimes you have to just laugh about it. There wasn't much chance of getting any laughs out of this particular customer.

Out of Order

Barney decided to call it a day. At least he had some nice Jelly Babies to eat on the journey home.

14

It was Saturday morning, and Barney was now regretting not swallowing his pride and asking Bowles if he could work some overtime this weekend. He hadn't anything planned all weekend except for a trip to the recycling centre, and he was desperate for the money. Today was the deadline he was given to pay £500. He had no idea what was going to happen. Maybe someone would just turn up at his front door and beat him up. Or more likely he was going to get jumped on walking down a dark alley. But he wasn't planning on walking down any dark alleys. Quite frankly he had no idea what to expect. He'd never been in this predicament before. It wasn't his world. So, the only thing he could do was carry on with his weekend as he normally would. Which was not doing a lot. Have a few beers and watch sport on the television. Phone his mum.

But someone phoned him first. It was Alison. That was unexpected. He spoke to her quite often when they were working, but this would be the first time they'd had any contact at the weekend. To be fair, he did say last time he saw her that she could call any time she wanted.

Alison didn't have much to say. She just needed to talk to someone, and Barney was all she had. Poor girl. No wonder he felt sorry for her if he was all she had.

She wasn't in a good way. The worry over her forthcoming eye test had turned into terror. The constant thoughts churning around in her head was making her feel ill.

Out of Order

Barney listened to her and tried to offer some sort of comfort, but he didn't really know what to tell her. He tried his best, but just repeating that she should try not to worry didn't feel like it was helping. He did consider asking her if she wanted to meet and go for a drink, or to the cinema or something. But he couldn't pluck up the courage to ask.

The call lasted twenty minutes and ended with Barney reminding her he would be with her on the day.

Returning to his own problems, he thought it was time to risk leaving the house. Whatever happens will happen. He had to go to the recycling centre anyway. He had changed a few fluorescent light tubes in some vending machines and needed to get rid of the faulty ones.

He walked boldly out to the car and found broken glass everywhere. A brick had been thrown through his windscreen. There was a note tied to it.

"YOU'VE MISSED THE DEADLINE. WE NOW WANT £1000 BY NEXT WEEKEND"

His initial reaction was one of shock, but that feeling didn't last long when he'd had time to think about it. If this was meant to frighten him it failed for two reasons. Firstly, they could attack his car all they wanted. It was a more favourable option than attacking him. It was a company car. He didn't have to pay anything towards it. He would just ring a number and someone would come to replace the glass. Secondly, it would be a lot easier to find a thousand pounds by next weekend than it would have been finding five hundred for this weekend, as it was payday before then. But he was just trying to convince himself everything was OK. It wasn't. They had upped their game. He considered calling the police. He knew it would be the right thing to do. But unfortunately, he was afraid it may result in some serious harm to him if he did.

He called the number for broken windscreens that was listed in a wallet inside the glove compartment, and someone turned up in less than two hours to fit a new one. It didn't take them too long to fit the new windscreen, but then they told him he couldn't drive it for 24 hours because the adhesive needed time to set. The trip to the recycling centre would have to wait until tomorrow. So, he just chilled out for the rest of the day. It was such an unusual situation he found himself in. Getting a brick thrown through his car window had made him feel a bit better and bought him a bit of time. But in reality, he was just fooling himself into thinking things would be OK.

He went out to his car the next morning and there didn't appear to be any fresh attacks, so he headed to the recycling centre. It wasn't something Barney was looking forward to. He was used to people getting hysterical when their Mars Bar didn't drop, or their change was 5p short. But recycling centre staff could be even worse than his customers. Put something in the wrong container and they treated you like you were some kind of evil monster. Also, to add to the ordeal, the council had started to charge for leaving certain items.

Out of Order

Not long ago he went there with a wooden chair and two long strips of wood. He was told it was fine to leave the chair, but to leave the two strips of wood would cost him £2.50 each. He wasn't given a reason for this, probably because there wasn't a rational explanation that anyone knew about. There was no way he was going to pay this, so he drove home, sawed the wood into small pieces, put them in bin bags, drove back to the recycling centre and threw them into the general rubbish skip. But he was proud to have done his bit to help the environment by recycling, even though, thanks to some jobsworth enforcing pointless rules, some recyclable wood had gone into landfill, not to mention eight miles of unnecessary exhaust fumes added to the air we breathe.

He was able to pull up at the correct bay, which made a nice change. He could see a container marked 'Light Tubes'. So, he picked up the ones he had and headed for the container, but was intercepted by one of the staff who looked ready to throw his weight about.

'Excuse me. Are those from household use or commercial use?'

'Household,' said Barney, which was a lie.

'How many have you got there?'

Barney made a deliberate show of counting them slowly.

'Five.'

'You're only allowed to leave four at a time.'

'What shall I do with the other one?'

'Take it away and bring it back another time.'

'Can't I just leave it this time and I'll learn my lesson never to do it again?'

'No. That's against the rules.'

'Can I walk out of the gate and come back in and leave it?'

'No. You're just abusing the system.'

'If I take it away, I'll probably just throw it in the bin. Wouldn't it be better if I leave it here?'

'I don't make the rules.'

'What if I had a hundred of them. Would it be good if I threw 96 of them in the bin? Or would I have to come back twenty-four times?'

'I'm afraid so. Unless you pay for the extra ones.'

'How much would I have to pay?'

'12p for every tube in excess of four.'

'So today that would be errrrm... hang on, give me a minute to work it out... 12p in total then?'

'That is correct.'

'I don't have any cash with me.' That was another lie, but there's no way he was going to give the man the satisfaction of getting him to pay. 'Would you take a cheque?'

'Not for 12p.'

'OK, you win. I'll leave just the four tubes and take the other one away, then I'll return another day to recycle it. Or I'll more likely just throw it in the bin. Which totally defeats the point of you having a recycling centre here. Well done mate. You're doing a splendid job.'

But it was futile saying anything more. The man was chuffed that he had carried out his duty to the letter. He wasn't going to let anyone take liberties with him.

He drove home trying to decide who was the biggest pain in the arse. The people who were demanding £1000, or the man who was demanding 12p?

15

Vendetta provided vending machines for a number of hospitals. Barney was often sent to big ones, such as Harefield Hospital, or Wexham Park Hospital, just north of Slough, plus a few smaller ones in the Windsor area. He hated hospitals. They made him squeamish and he didn't like watching patients being wheeled about. Back in his Hot Cup days he was repairing a vending machine in a waiting room at Great Ormond Street hospital, which is a famous children's hospital in Central London. While he was trying to work, a man and a woman were crying loudly and inconsolably. He never knew the precise reason, and preferred not to, but it was no doubt something not very pleasant concerning their child. It disturbed him, and he never forgot it all these years later.

Alison also visited those same hospitals to restock the machines. She didn't have the same dread of hospitals that Barney had. To her it was just another customer. Harefield hospital was on her schedule today.

It wasn't easy for Alison to focus on her job. There was only one thing on her mind. It was with her constantly all day and all night. It was causing her to feel nauseous and she could feel some pains in her chest. At her lowest moments he even had a few cigarettes, and she was disgusted with herself for doing so. It had been two weeks since her visit to the opticians. It felt much longer. And the next four weeks would feel like a lifetime.

Out of Order

She was restocking a coffee machine in the waiting room of the accident and emergency department in the hospital. On many occasions Alison had loaded this machine while people in a bad way were wheeled past on trolleys. Usually she didn't bat an eyelid, but today it was making her feel uneasy. In fact, she realised she wasn't feeling very well at all.

She could feel a pain in her chest. But this time it wasn't just a feeling. It was more severe. She dropped everything and sat down on a chair. The room was full of people with various illnesses and injuries waiting to be seen. She was just sitting there desperate for the pain to go away. If it had been anywhere else, she would have been noticed and someone could have helped her. But she knew that if something was seriously wrong with her, an A&E department of a hospital was the best place to be.

After a few minutes she thought it was time to get the attention of one of the staff. She tried to stand up and was about to approach the reception. But much to her relief the pain eased. In a few minutes it had gone altogether. She sat down again for a few more minutes, then slowly got up and went back to the coffee machine to finish her work. Then she closed the machine, took a coffee and sat back down to drink it. She felt fine now and tried to make sense of what had just happened. She knew she ought to go to the doctors and get checked out. It was probably nothing, but best to be on the safe side. Then again, she already had her eye problems, and it wasn't a good time to be having any other health scares.

She was feeling a lot better now. She finished her coffee and went back to the van.

Her next job was in a large supermarket two miles away. That would be handy. She could do her shopping while she was there. It might be a good idea to buy some painkillers while she was there just in case. Or some indigestion tablets.

But as she was pushing her trolley around the shop it happened again. Even more severe. There was no messing about this time. She shouted out to a young man stacking shelves. All that she managed to get out was, 'I need help!'

The young man could tell from the way she was slumped over her trolly that she wasn't asking for help finding the pasta sauce. He ran to get his manager and the two of them helped her to a seat in an empty room. Then they dialled 999.

The voice on the other end of the phone took a few details from the manager, then asked to speak to the patient. He handed the phone to Alison who by now was in excruciating pain and could barely talk. The first thing she heard was that there was an ambulance on its way. She was asked to describe the symptoms, which she did as best she could. Then the voice on the phone asked if she could get some aspirins. The young shelf stacker was sent to the medicine department and came back with a box. Alison was instructed to swallow three tablets. She supposed that if an A&E department of a hospital was the best place for something like this to happen, then a supermarket has to be second.

The two men sat with her until the ambulance arrived, which seemed like hours, but was much closer to twenty minutes, then after a brief assessment she was taken to Wexham Park Hospital.

The next few hours dragged on slowly. There were many tests

and taking of tablets, but she was mainly lying around doing nothing. The chest pains would come and go, and every time it got a bit too uncomfortable, a nurse would spray something under her tongue, and that usually eased it.

She'd called Mary at the office, who responded with, 'Fucking hell Alison!'

But then she became rather more helpful. First, she arranged for the van to be collected from the supermarket car park. Then she passed on the news to Allison's supervisor.

The supervisor phoned Alison and when she realised, as she already suspected, Alison wouldn't have anyone to visit her, she drove to the hospital that evening and sat with her for three hours.

By then she had been told she'd had a mild heart attack and would be kept in for a day or two.

Mild? If that was mild, she wouldn't much relish having a medium one.

After her supervisor had gone home, she lay awake thinking life had not been kind to her of late. Since finding the courage to get out of her dreadful marriage which had worn her down and made her feel worthless, she had worked hard to get back to being the strong and feisty person she used to be. She had lost weight, and given up smoking. A bit too late? Or maybe in the nick of time. But although smoking and being overweight were no doubt influential on today's events, she had no doubt in her own mind stress had brought this on. She wasn't feeling strong and feisty as she lay there. She was feeling that she'd made a lot of effort for nothing. She was lonely. She'd lost touch with all of her friends. The closest she had to a friend was Barney. She liked him, although she thought he was a bit weird. It would be nice if he would visit her. Does he even know she is there? Why was she thinking about him so much?

16

'Oh no! Not another school!'

Barney had a flashback to the time when he was intimidated by a gang of teenage schoolgirls and walked into a wall.

But he needn't have worried. The school he was sent to this time was a primary school, much to his relief. Surely, he could cope with a few kids of that age.

The machine was in an open space which was deserted and silent. It made such a pleasant change to be able to just get on with the job without being hassled.

He was progressing nicely, when a group of around fifteen kids who must have been about 6 or 7 years old, surrounded him and all sat on the floor with their arms folded and their legs crossed. They were completely silent and stared at him. This was really creepy. It was even more unnerving than the gang of teenage girls. He completely lost his focus and was struggling to complete the job. Even more concerning was he needed to go back to the car for a part. He didn't know how he was going to get past them.

One of the girls put her hand in the air and he was relieved when she broke the silence, 'Sir. What are you doing?'

He wasn't used to being called 'Sir', and it gave him a confidence boost.

'Get a grip lad', he thought to himself. 'You're the adult here'.

If he'd been asked the same question by an adult, he would have said something along the lines of, 'I'm tuning a bloody piano. What does it look like I'm doing?'

But because he was asked by a seven-year-old girl, who may one day grow up to become an evil bitch, but at the moment was all sweetness and innocence, he answered her in the softest voice he could manage.

'I'm mending the machine. It's broken.'

'Why's it broken, sir?'

'Umm. Well err, one of the TRIACs on the I/O PCB has burnt out. Erm. Well, you see, the TRIAC switches the voltage to the motor which errrrm… No. What I mean is, the Kit Kats are stuck.'

'How do you unstuck them sir?'

He was relieved to see a teacher approach and tell them, 'Come along boys and girls. It's time to get back to class.'

They all stood up and hurried off.

He felt instantly at ease when he was left on his own. He had never really got on with children. There were none in his family and he'd never had any strong desire to have any of his own. He sometimes wondered if he would have made a good dad. He doubted if he would have the patience required. But that was all academic now. He was at an age where it was unlikely to happen. Not that it bothered him.

Now that he was no longer surrounded, he could walk back to the car to pick up a new I/O board.

Out of Order

He fitted the replacement board, did a few test vends and left, taking with him a 'test' KitKat as comfort food to help him recover from the ordeal.

Just as he was arriving back at the car his phone rang. The display read 'Sweary'.

'Hello Mary. What a pleasure it is to hear from you, as always.'

'Don't be fucking sarcastic with me. I'm calling to ask if you'll do me a little favour Barney.'

'Oh no. I don't like the sound of that.'

'Don't worry. It's nothing much. A customer needs a price change on his coffee machine. Alison was due to do it this morning, but obviously she can't now.'

Barney was puzzled. 'What's obvious? Why can't Alison do it?'

'Oh! Haven't you heard?'

'Evidently not. Heard what exactly?'

'She had a heart attack yesterday. She's in Wexham Park Hospital.'

Barney was stunned. 'Oh. Right. Of course I'll do it.'

'Thanks. You're a star.'

Barney sat in his car doing nothing for a while. At first, he was feeling angry that nobody had told him. But then again why would they? She was just someone who worked for the same company as him who's paths crossed occasionally.

He was surprised at how bad he was feeling about it. Obviously, he felt sorry for her, especially all this on top of the trouble with her eyes. Maybe he ought to visit her. But he didn't know if it was the right thing to do.

He didn't feel like doing any more work today. But he would have to do the price change that Alison was meant to do. That didn't take very long, then he made a decision. He would go and visit her.

But work intervened yet again. He received a job, with a note saying 'must be done today', which was thirty miles in the wrong direction. The fault description was an intriguing one. It simply said 'unplug machine'.

It took 45 minutes to travel to the site. He reported to the reception.

'Good afternoon. Can I help you?'

'Hi I'm from Vendetta. I'm here to do some work on your vending machine, but I'm a little unclear exactly what it is you want me to do.'

'I'll just call someone. Take a seat.'

So, Barney sat down and waited there impatiently for ten minutes until a man turned up.

He introduced himself and told Barney, as it was his first time here, he would need to watch a site induction video and answer some health and safety questions. And finally, before he was allowed to work, he would be required to fill in a risk assessment form.

He had done several of these before. He would be forced to

watch a video for about twenty minutes, then answer questions such as 'What should you wear on your feet for protection? A: Steel toe capped safety boots. B: Sandals. C: Flip flops.'

He completed the test with a 100% pass mark, and thought that anyone who doesn't get 100% on this test shouldn't be allowed to leave the house. Or even be left alone in the house.

He wasn't questioning whether his job had the potential to harm him. He remembered years ago hearing that more people were killed by vending machines than sharks every year. He had received many cuts, burns, bruises and electric shocks over the years. Then there was the time when a television set fell on him as he opened a vending machine door. He had got away with just a cut on his head. A first aider stuck a plaster over it and then insisted he filled in an accident report form. There was a list of daft questions, one of which was, 'Do you feel there was anything that could have been done to prevent the accident?'

Barney wrote 'Yes. Don't put a fucking television set on top of the vending machine!'

The man led him to the machine.

'What is it that you want me to do?'

'Unplug the machine.'

Barney was puzzled.

'Pardon?'

'Just unplug the machine.'

'You mean just pull the mains plug out of the wall socket?'

'Yes please. We're moving the machine while the wall gets painted.'

'Why couldn't one of you have just unplugged it. It hardly requires a qualified engineer.'

'Nobody would do it.'

'Why couldn't you do it?'

'It's not my responsibility.'

'But it's your responsibility to arrange for someone else to do it?'

'Yes.'

'So, let me get this straight. I've driven thirty miles. I've been sitting in the reception for ten minutes. I've spent twenty minutes watching a site induction video. Sat a health and safety test. And filled in a risk assessment form. Just to pull a plug out?'

'Yes.'

There was nothing more Barney wanted to add. He unplugged the plug and got out of there as quickly as he could. He set off for the hospital.

Due to some traffic problems, it took more than an hour to get there. He found a space in the car park after driving around it for ten minutes, then went to the machine to buy a ticket. The cost of parking was surprisingly expensive. Usually when he parked there to do a job, he didn't take much notice of how much it cost, because the company would pay. He thought about putting it through with his regular parking expenses claim. Nobody would know. But what if Bowles was scrutinising everything he was doing. Waiting for him to make a slip-up. Then he could fire him for defrauding the company. No, he decided it would be better not to risk it.

He wandered into the reception and walked past a trio of vending machines that he had worked on several times. It made him feel quite proud to see these machines working, and people happily using them. He found the ward Alison was in and the nurse directed him to where she lay.

She initially looked horrified to see him.

'Hello Alison. Sorry to just turn up like this, but I thought you might need a visitor.'

Even though she was delighted to see him, she didn't want to show it. 'I didn't want anyone to see me like this. I must look a right mess?'

'Oh, don't worry about that.'

'So, you're saying I do look a right mess?'

'No. That's not what I'm saying at all. You look great. How are you?

'I'm feeling fine. It's like it never happened. I just want to go home. But they say I've got to stay here tonight and can go home tomorrow.'

They chatted for almost two hours. He described his ridiculous day at work. How he had to drive miles because nobody would pull a plug out. How he was freaked out by a bunch of primary school children.

'So, don't you like kids then?' she asked.

It's not that I don't like them. I don't have many dealings with them, so I'm not too sure how to behave around them. Especially when there are lots of them surrounding me, staring at me in silence. One of them asked me what was wrong with the machine and I answered her as if I was talking to a professor of physics at Cambridge University.'

She laughed briefly. Then her expression turned to sadness. 'I love kids,' she said.

'Didn't you want to have any of your own then?' he asked rather tactlessly.

'Yes. Desperately. But my ex-husband didn't want any. And whatever he wanted was what we did. It was probably for the best. He would have been a control freak to the children too. He would have made their lives a misery as well as mine.'

'What about now. Do you still have any ambitions to be a mum?'

'I think it's too late. I'm not getting any younger. Besides, I'm on my own now. And I've now got something wrong with my heart. And I'm in danger of losing my eyesight. Not an ideal situation to be having children.'

Barney felt uneasy and was relieved when she changed the subject.

She described how the events of the heart attack unfolded, which wasn't pleasant to listen to either. He told her he was going to Torquay for training tomorrow. She told him she was even more worried about her eyes. He told her to stop worrying or she might give herself a heart attack. Not his best ever joke.

Out of Order

He attempted to change the subject yet again. 'Did I ever tell you about the job I once did in Northwick Park hospital?'

'No. I don't think so.'

'I was working on a machine in a corridor, when I was suddenly barged to the ground by a gang of men fighting. I got my leg trapped underneath them as they wrestled on the ground. It turned out to be three security staff trying to restrain one man who had gone berserk. They got up without saying a word to me and led him away, leaving me sprawled out on the floor.'

'That could only happen to you.' she said.

'I don't know about that. Given your recent run of bad luck, it would be more likely to happen to you.'

After checking she didn't need anything bringing in, or needed a lift home tomorrow (all already sorted by her supervisor) he wished her well and headed for home.

He wanted to be more helpful to her. She'd had a tough life. Her ex-husband sounded truly horrible. Now she's got all these health issues. And here he was adding to her misery by blabbing on about having kids.

And on the subject of adding to someone's misery, Colin called him as he was driving home. That's all he needed. Reluctantly he put him on loudspeaker so he could keep driving.

'Hiya Barn. How's it going?'

'Alright Colin.'

'So, what's happening with you?'

'Nothing.'

'I've got to go on a training course next week for that Cafeblam 73. It's in Torquay.'

Barney froze. 'Oh no, please. You can't do this to me.'

He never said that sentence out loud. He only mumbled it. Instead, he asked, 'When are you going?'

'Wednesday.'

A wave of relief surged through Barney. 'Oh, that's a shame. I'm going on Friday. We could have gone in one car.'

'What do you know about the Cafeblam 73, Barn?'

'Sorry Colin. Somebody is trying to call me. I need to answer it.'

Then he switched his phone off.

17

Pay day had arrived, but most of it was instantly gone to pay the thousand pounds demanded by the people he owed money to. That took the money owed down to six thousand, but he wouldn't have much left to see him through the month. Not that Barney should need to spend any money today. He was going to a hotel in Torquay tonight, so he would be having a meal and a few beers at the company's expense.

He had to get to the hotel before five o'clock to attend an introduction meeting with his fellow trainees and with the people who manufactured the Cafeblam 73. This meant that he had permission to finish work at two o'clock to give himself time to get there. That wasn't giving him much of a margin for error, so he would probably aim to get away before one o'clock. Providing his day went smoothly and trouble free. Predictably it didn't.

He came face to face with a customer whose mannerisms were just like somebody who he could expect to encounter later that evening as a manager of a hotel in Torquay. Barney was very tempted to call him Basil.

'Hello. I'm from Vendetta. I'm here to…'

Basil interrupted rather bluntly.

'Will you fix this machine?'

'That's why I'm here. What's it doing wrong?'

'No cups are coming out.'

Barney selected a coffee, which was duly dispensed and casually took a few sips. He desperately wanted to do a version of one of Fawlty's classic moments. 'I believe this is the cup sir, between the table and the sky.'

Instead, he opted for, 'Well it seems OK to me.'

This got Basil even more agitated and he started waving his arms about.

'Well it is now, but it wasn't yesterday.'

Barney decided a normal polite approach would be wasted on this man. 'That's handy, because I'm a time traveller.'

'Is there something wrong with you?'

'With me? I'm not sure. I do seem to attract my unfair share of cranks. More to the point, is there something wrong with your coffee machine?'

'Yes, there is. It wasn't dispensing cups yesterday. Then one of your Vendetta colleagues visited. Then all of a sudden it was dispensing cups. It doesn't make sense.'

'I've worked on vending machines for many years, but this is a really tricky one. I do have a theory though. Could it be that it had possibly run out of cups, and the person who visited put some more in?'

Basil paused for a while and considered this. 'Yes, I suppose that could be the case.'

'I think we will assume that it is. Especially as that is a crucial part of my colleague's role. Is it doing anything else wrong?'

'No. I don't believe so.'

Mr. Fawlty was placated by this explanation and returned to

Out of Order

whatever planet he was living on. Barney made his escape, trying to decide which category to file this one under. He wasn't the standard angry customer just looking for someone to have a go at. He wasn't one of the out and out sarcastic or rude types. Barney decided he was just bonkers. He drove away wondering just how many more crackpots there were left on the planet he was still yet to meet. The answer to that was at least one. The one he was on his way to meet next.

Barney had long thought that there must be some sort of mathematical formula which could explain why things are more likely to go wrong when you're in a hurry. It had happened to him so many times, and was about to happen to him again today.

The job was at one of his regular customers. It was a large factory in Denham that made some sort of engineering components for military aircraft. Barney usually enjoyed visiting this place. There were photographs of aeroplanes all over a large wall, and he would normally spend a bit of time looking at them. But not today. He didn't have time. The vending machine was in the middle of the factory floor. It was always noisy and busy. The task he faced was a relatively easy one. It was just a matter of removing a faulty coin controller and fitting a new one, then transferring coins from one to the other. So, he was optimistic that he would be able to set off on his long drive nice and early.

Things started off normally and trouble free. He removed the faulty coin controller and put it on a bench next to his tool bag. The coin controller is a device that takes in the coins which have been inserted into the vending machine, tells the machine how much credit to display, then sorts the coins into various change tubes, before finally dispensing any change the buyer is entitled to.

At this point Barney had a sudden need to pay a visit to the gents. He was gone for less than two minutes. On his return he fitted the new controller, which just left him the final task of taking the coins from the old one to fill the tubes in the new one. But the old one wasn't there anymore.

Barney was distraught. There must have been more than a hundred pounds worth of coins in there. And the value of the unit itself was even more than that. This could be big trouble for him. If he didn't get it back, this would be the excuse that Bowles would need to get rid of him at last.

A man working on a nearby workbench was watching him.

'Have you lost something mate?'

Barney tried to keep his cool. If this man saw what happened, he needed to be friendly to him. 'Yes. Something very important.'

The man told him, 'The cleaner picked something up and threw it in his rubbish bag while you were gone.'

'Oh terrific! Do you know which way he went?'

The man pointed down a long corridor. Barney ran off in pursuit.

It was a big factory. The cleaner had a ten-minute head start on him, because he was too busy fitting the new one to notice soon enough that the old one had gone.

He ran around the factory in a panic, and eventually found the cleaner sitting down in a refreshment area having a cup of tea. He continued with the friendly approach.

'Excuse me. I think you may have picked up something belonging to me.'

'I'm afraid it's too late now. The sacks have been tied up'

Barney continued to be friendly, but it was through gritted teeth.

'It is an expensive piece of equipment. It is essential I have it back.'

'Well unfortunately it's too late. You shouldn't have left it lying around.'

That was enough to switch Barney from polite mode to angry. He pulled a Stanley knife out of his pocket. Then the volume of his voice increased dramatically.

'I didn't leave it lying around. I was working on it. I was gone for two minutes and you took it. And I'm taking it back, whether you like it or not. If you don't open the bag, I'll cut it open.'

The cleaner instantly changed his attitude. He was facing an angry man wielding a knife. He opened the bag and removed the unit. It was covered in some kind of gooey, smelly substance. Barney politely thanked the cleaner, sarcastically and stormed off.

After cleaning the coin controller, and himself, he took the coins and fed them into the machine. The machine added up the coins as they went in. £106.45 worth. Almost thrown out with the rubbish.

Outside in the cool air he pondered on how lucky he had been considering the possible alternative outcomes. If he hadn't found the cleaner, he would have been well and truly up the creek. On the other hand, if the cleaner had stuck to his guns and refused to open the bag, things could have got messy for him, both literally and metaphorically. He pictured the look on Richard Bowles face when he took the phone call.

'Your engineer has gone on the rampage with a knife. He has thrown rubbish everywhere, and we've had to send our cleaner home because he's traumatised.'

He was hugely relieved to get away from the place, but the time wasted meant he was later setting off than he had planned. He hit the M4 half an hour behind schedule.

18

Despite the shenanigans with the cleaner, Barney had quite a good journey to Devon. There was always potential for traffic jams on the M4 and M5, especially around the Bristol area, but it hadn't been too bad today. It had got slow after he had left the motorway and was working his way through the town towards the sea front, but that was to be expected. It wasn't anything like the London rush hours he'd been stuck in many times, but his arrival coincided with people leaving work, so it was a bit of a drag.

After checking in to his very nice hotel, he had half an hour to spare before he was due to meet the others. He was tempted to pop into the bar, but decided to do the sensible thing and leave the drinking until after the get together. So, he went for a stroll along the beach instead.

The hotel was in a superb location on the seafront, and Barney wished he had been sent here in July instead of November. But it was very pleasant all the same. He liked being next to the sea. He often dreamed of having a house overlooking the sea. Some of the houses here, built into the hills climbing high above the water were magnificent. He would never be able to afford anything like that.

The training was taking place in the actual hotel, which was unusual. It would normally be held at the manufacturer's factory or office. At least this way he wouldn't have far to travel. He headed back there at five o'clock. In the car park he spotted a Vendetta van. It was good to know there was someone else from his company on the course too. Maybe they could have a few pints together later.

Barney couldn't see the point in having this introductory meeting. There were eight others taking the course, plus the trainer and his assistant. Everybody told everybody else their names and which company they worked for. But he never took any notice of their names, and tended to invent nicknames for them all based on their characteristics, and he had no interest in which company they worked for. The trainer, who was called Phil, waffled on for ten minutes about the schedule for the following day. He used a lot of euphemisms and annoying phrases which didn't make much sense.

'Well, that's all for tonight. I'm just going outside to turn the horse around, then I'll be popping into the bar for a drink if anyone wants to wet their whistle with me? Then we can put a few marbles in the jar and give them a good shake.'

It was going to be a tough day tomorrow if that was how he was going to talk. But Barney understood the bit about going to the bar and was ready for a drink.

The first one to talk to him in the bar was the trainer's assistant. His standout feature was a huge yellow spot on the end of his nose. Barney found this too distracting, and he couldn't take in a single word he was saying because he was just mentally squeezing the spot.

He wasn't too good at socialising at events such as this. He usually found most of the others boring, and only interested in talking about work. He decided the best strategy would be to seek out the other Vendetta employee, who turned out to be a woman eight years younger than him, and very good looking too, although he found her scouse accent hard to understand at first, and had to occasionally nod in agreement and bluff his way through.

They had briefly met at the introduction. She was an operator who was training to be an engineer working from the Liverpool office.

She had gone back to her room to have a shower and change out of uniform. She had been working on the morning and was feeling a bit grimy from the effects of cleaning coffee machines. When she came down to the bar, she was wearing tight jeans and a red top, and she had taken her blonde hair out of a ponytail. Barney thought she looked stunning.

The ten others were sitting in a large circle and Barney sat down between Attractive Scouse Vendetta Woman and the Brummie Sniffer. He made a mental note to avoid sitting too near the Brummie Sniffer tomorrow if he could help it.

All of the others in the group were men. After an hour of mundane chatter about vending machines, Euphemism Man and Yellow Zit Nose announced their departure.

'We're off to climb the wooden hill to Bedfordshire. See you in the morning at nine bells. Don't forget to water the cactus.'

Barney just wanted to stand up and scream, 'What the hell are you talking about?', but managed to restrain himself.

Four of the others left soon after that leaving five of them. The quality of the conversation was dire. There were so many subjects that would have interested Barney. Sport, for instance, or music. Maybe a bit of politics. But no. All this lot were interested in were vending machines.

He had to get out of there. Not least because he was very soon going to yell at the man sitting next to him, 'Oh for Christ's sake, get a tissue and blow your fucking nose!'

He needed an excuse to leave. He wanted to try the pub just a little way along the seafront, but didn't want any of the others to come with him.

He got the feeling Attractive Scouse Vendetta Woman was getting as bored as he was. He chatted to her for a while. None of the others could hear. They were too busy discussing the merits of the Scoffatron 37 food machine.

He said to her, 'I can't stand this any longer. I'm thinking of going for a drink somewhere else.'

This perked her up a bit. 'Oh, do you mind if I come with you?'

'Not at all. What shall we tell this lot?'

'Nothing. Sod them. Let's just go,' she said.

And, they did. They just stood up and walked out. They wandered along to the pub he had spotted earlier.

It was a pub very much to his liking. Some good music playing, sport on the television, a pool table, and some tempting snacks. They even had a dartboard, which reminded him he was missing the match tonight. He didn't suppose she played darts. He was correct on that one, but she did like pool, and they had a few games, after which they sat down to have some food and yet more drinks.

Out of Order

It was difficult not to talk about work as it was the first subject they knew they had in common, which made it an obvious starting point. But they avoided talking about actual vending machines and stuck to gossip about their staff and customers. It sounded like there was a big difference between the customers in Liverpool and the ones in Slough.

He asked her, 'Why do you want to be an engineer instead of an operator?'

'More money. A bit of variety in the work. A car instead of a van. All the same reasons you want to be one.'

He told her, 'It can be a pain sometimes. And the customers can be an even bigger pain, although the ones up your way sound a lot more friendly than some of the ones I have to deal with.'

'I already know that. But I think I'd be good at it. I already do quite a few of the easier repairs myself. I might as well get paid for it. Besides, I want to prove that women can do the job just as successfully as men. I get the feeling my boss is against the idea. He's a bit of a dinosaur.'

It just occurred to Barney that he'd never worked with a female engineer in the twenty-two years he'd been doing the job.

'He must think you can do it. Otherwise, why would he send you on this training?'

'Because he thinks I will find it too difficult and will give up the idea. But I won't.'

'I must warn you though, you get sent to some really stupid jobs.'

'I can imagine. Have you got any good stories to tell?'

Barney tried to think of a good example. 'There was a man who trapped his arm in a canned drink vending machine. His can of cola didn't drop. He reached in to try and get it out and got stuck. He was stuck there for over an hour. When they opened the door, they saw he was holding on to a can. If he'd let go of it his arm would have come out.'

She laughed loudly.

'That happened to Homer Simpson! Tell me a real one.'

Barney laughed too.

'OK. This one is real. Just before Christmas last year I was given a call in Brunel University in West London. The reported fault was 'vending machine is upside down.' A bunch of students had turned a machine upside down as an end of term prank. I don't know how they did it. It was a huge machine. Those things are really heavy. There must have been a lot of them. I'm not sure what they expected me to do about it.'

She said, 'We operators get our share of daft stuff too. Only a few weeks ago I was sent to one of our customers who had reported that there was a bird trapped in the machine. I was the nearest to them at the time and they wanted me to let it out. When I got there, it did sound a bit like a bird chirping. It was caused by a squeaky extraction fan. A quick squirt of WD40 cured it. I told the customer I had killed the bird to stop it chirping. Because they were so gullible, I got a bit carried away. I described how I'd half drowned it in the drip bucket, then finished it off by chopping its head off with a chisel. They believed me. They had a go at me and said I could have just let it fly away instead of killing it. One of them even phoned our office to say they were disgusted with me.'

Barney was impressed.

'I like your style. You're going to make a good engineer.'

'Thanks.'

'Good luck. I hope it all works out for you.'

Then they moved on to various other subjects and as the beers continued to flow, Barney was feeling attracted to her. He was even finding her Liverpool accent sexy. She had noticed his interest in her and was becoming more and more flirty.

They were having a great time, and eleven o'clock came around very quickly. By now they were pretty drunk. They could have happily stayed there all night, but the barman had announced closing time.

Barney suggested having another drink in the hotel bar which was open until midnight. She agreed. Hopefully the rest of the group would have gone to bed by now. Then they wandered back along the seafront, wobbling a bit, and she held on to his arm.

The others had gone. The bar was virtually empty. He got the drinks from the bar, paid for by Vendetta, and took them to a table. But she didn't sit down. He wasn't expecting what she said next.

'Shall we take the drinks back to my room?'

He was momentarily rendered speechless. She noticed his hesitation, and said, 'What's wrong. Don't you want to?'

In his excitement he was struggling to string together a sentence. 'I... err, I... no. I mean yes. Of course I want to. Are you mad? Who wouldn't?'

Then he realised he didn't sound cool and tried to stop babbling. Despite his excitement, he remembered that he had to take a tablet.

'I've just got to pop back to my room for something. I'll see you in a minute.'

'OK. I'm in room 347.'

He dashed off to his room and took his tablet. He decided it might be a good idea to see if he had any condoms. He rummaged through his toiletry bag and found some. They were two years past their use by date, a sad reflection on how successful he'd been with women in recent times, but he would take the chance anyway. He assumed they would still work, and she was hardly likely to check the date.

Then he was virtually running along the corridor to find her room. What an unexpected bonus this was. He'd been having a tough time recently, but finally a bit of good luck had come his way.

He found room 307 and tapped on the door. A large man opened the door. and didn't look happy.

'Yes? What do you want? This had better be important. I was asleep, and I've got an early start in the morning.'

Barney was confused. Why was this man in her room?

'Sorry. I'm looking for my work colleague.'

'Well, your work colleague isn't here. Now fuck off unless you want a punch in the face.'

Out of Order

Barney got away from there as quickly as possible. He must have gone to the wrong room. But which one was the right room? He was sure she'd said 307. Maybe it was 207? But he couldn't go around knocking on doors randomly at this time of night.

He was beginning to panic. But then he had an idea. He went to the hotel reception.

'Sorry to bother you, but I am staying here with a work colleague. I have some important paperwork I need to give her tonight, but I can't remember what room she's in.'

'I can't just give you her room number.'

'OK. I can understand that. But would it be possible for you to contact her and check that it would be alright to give me her room number?'

'Can't you ring her mobile phone?'

'I don't have her number.'

'Alright. I'll call the telephone in her room. What room is she in?'

'I don't know what room she's in. That's what I'm trying to find out.'

'Oh yes of course. Sorry. What's her name?'

'Erm… I'm not sure.'

'You don't know her name either? Are you sure she's your work colleague?'

'Yes. She is.'

'I sorry, I can't help you any further. I think you need to go back to your own room. Otherwise, I will be forced to call the manager.'

Barney didn't have any choice. If the manager called Richard Bowles, and told him one of his staff had been running around his hotel at midnight, drunk, and trying to get into a woman's room, he might have the chance he needed to fire him at last. And he would be a laughing stock with everyone else at work.

Barney was distraught. He wandered into the bar and ordered another beer. He sat there for a while in the hope that she would come back down to find him. But she didn't reappear. He finished his beer and reluctantly returned to his room alone. He was tempted to bang on 307 again and get beaten up. He deserved it.

19

Getting through the day was not going to be easy for Barney. He was feeling quite ill, caused by the large amounts of beer he had consumed. He would probably throw up when he had to listen to the man who kept sniffing his snots back in. He would have to listen to Know All and Knows Even More pointing out useless facts and asking stupid questions to try and impress the instructor. He'd have to listen to the instructor who speaks in euphemisms and nonsensical phrases. He'd have to take instructions from the assistant with the huge yellow spot on his nose that needed squeezing. But worst of all he would have to face the woman who he could have had gone to bed with if he hadn't forgotten her room number, or had bothered to learn her name.

First of all, he had to face breakfast. He wasn't feeling at all hungry, but he felt he ought to eat something, and the company was paying for it. So he forced himself to get dressed and found his way to the restaurant.

He found Attractive Scouse Vendetta Woman sitting at a table on her own. She didn't look too happy to see him. He decided it would be better to go to her and get his explanation done straight away.

'Do you mind if I join you?'

'Oh, so you want to join me. That will make a nice change.'

He assumed that meant yes, he could sit down, so he went to the buffet to collect some breakfast. On his return she said, 'Oh, you came back! I wasn't expecting you.'

'Alright, alright. You've made your point. I feel bad enough already. Would you mind going easy on me now?'

He might as well tell the truth, even thought it would sound pretty pathetic.

'I'm really sorry.' That must have been the understatement of the century. 'I must have misheard when you told me your room number. I knocked on the wrong door and almost got a good hiding.'

She found that very funny and laughed out loud. He thought it would be better to keep quiet about the part where he didn't know her name. She was unlikely to find that quite so funny.

He told her, 'If it's any consolation, I'm going to be kicking myself for the rest of my life every time I remember it.'

'Never mind,' She said, 'At least we had a good night out.'

'Yes, we did. I don't suppose you'd like to stay for another night?'

'I'd love to. But I don't know how I'd explain it to my husband and kids. I told them I'd only be away for one night.'

She was married. Something else he didn't know about her other than her name. His change in luck hadn't lasted very long.

They finished breakfast and headed to the room where the training was taking place. The others were already there waiting eagerly. Phil and his assistant arrived.

'Good morning everybody. Time to put the gunpowder into the cannon.'

He had started already. Barney didn't have a clue what he meant by that.

'Right. Let the dog see the rabbit. Has everybody got their hats on straight?'

Nor that.

Yellow Zit Nose then wheeled out the machine, and everyone got their first glimpse of the Cafeblam 73.

'How does this baby fly your kite?' said Phil. 'This is the Rolls Royce of the coffee machine world.'

Barney was suitably unimpressed. The coffee machines already in existence made perfectly good coffee. OK, so they broke down more often than they should, but if they didn't, he would be out of a job.

The first two hours dragged over. At eleven o'clock Phil announced, 'Well I'm just popping out to shake hands with my best mate. We'll take a break. Grab yourselves a coffee and I'll see you back here in twenty doodahs.'

Barney got himself a tea in a plastic cup and took it outside to drink sitting next to the sea, hypnotised by the waves going in and out. He was thinking this training was a complete waste of time and wanted it to end.

He finished his tea and went back inside. The trainer hadn't returned. He eventually came back and apologised, 'Sorry I'm late back. I had to lay a cable.'

Barney already had a weak stomach, and tried desperately to put the image out of his head. There were a few more of those throughout the rest of the day, plus the predictable bullshit from

Know All and Knows Even More, and the Brummie Sniffer made himself heard, even from the other side of the room. The assistant still hadn't squeezed his yellow spot.

When they reached the end of the day, he was handing out manuals. He was announcing something which may, or may not have been important, but Barney didn't hear a word. That spot was getting bigger. He could have sworn he saw it actually growing, and was going to burst all over him any minute now. He had given him the benefit of the doubt yesterday there was a possibility he didn't know about it. But surely when he was in the bathroom brushing his teeth or washing his face last night or this morning, he couldn't have missed it. Why hadn't he popped it? He handed each of them a manual for the Cafeblam 73. It contained circuit diagrams, programming instructions, a list of spare part numbers, a fault-finding guide, plus a phone number for technical help. This was all he needed if he was sent to repair one. Why couldn't they have just sent him all this in the first place and saved the trouble of dragging him all the way down to Devon?

Phil gave one final outburst of nonsense, 'Don't forget. When you're out there in the trenches, don't look at the problem. Look all around the problem. But now it's time to saddle up the horses and head for the mountains.'

Barney agreed. He called in to the gents to shake hands with his own best mate, then went out to saddle up his horse. He took one last stroll along the beach before getting in the car.

On the drive home he couldn't help reflect on what might have been. He was feeling down. But it wasn't just because he'd messed up that was bothering him. He was feeling down ever since he found out she was married. If she'd been single, there was a chance she would have stayed an extra night. Or even if she wasn't able to, he could have asked for her phone number and got in touch with her. Then have a stopover in Liverpool on his next trip to the Lake District.

Halfway through his journey home he stopped at the motorway services. While he was there, he gave Roy a call.

'How did it go last night?'

'We won 8-3. It was a brilliant performance from the whole team. Especially Bob who took your place.'

'Great. You know how to cheer me up. Does that mean I won't get back in the team?'

'No. Bob only wants to play when we're short. So, if you want to play next week, you're in.'

'OK. Put me down. Where are we playing?'

'We're at home. We're playing Norfolk and Good again. We drew them in the cup. It will probably be our last game before Christmas, so we'll make it a really good session.'

'Yes. That's just what I could do with right now.'

'Did you not get the chance to have a drink in Torquay then?'

'Oh yes. I had a great night out in a cracking pub with a beautiful woman. But ruined things with my own stupidity.'

Roy laughed. 'Why doesn't that surprise me? What did you do this time?'

'I don't want to talk about it.'

20

It had been one of the toughest weeks Barney had ever had to endure. On top of the self-inflicted misery of Torquay, nothing seemed to be going right for him. He wasn't getting sent many easy jobs. It seemed to him that everywhere he went on Monday and Tuesday he had problems. There were machines he couldn't fix, which he hated, and jobs which left him covered in all kinds of mess and cuts and bruises, and smelling of sour milk. Plus of course he was constantly dealing with people who weren't respectful to him.

He woke up on Wednesday morning not feeling much like going to work. As he headed out of the door, he spotted a blank envelope lying on the doormat. His immediate thoughts were that it was going to be a new threat and demand for more money. But it wasn't anything like that. The envelope contained a leaflet from his local leisure centre. It was a promotional offer for a free session at their swimming pool and spa.

He wasn't too enthusiastic about it. He hadn't been swimming for a few years and didn't particularly feel inclined to go. Maybe he could offer the voucher to Liam, who liked to keep fit. Or Alison. She regularly visited the gym, but he didn't know if she liked to go swimming.

He completed his first two jobs, which thankfully were easy for a change, then he called Liam.

'Alright Barney.'

'Alright. Liam. I was sent a voucher for a free two-hour session at my local pool and spa. I won't be using it. You can have it if you want.'

'Yeah okay. When's it for?'

'It has to be used this week.'

'Oh, in that case I can't do it. I've got things on every evening.'

'Okay, not to worry. I just thought I'd ask. I'll see if Alison wants it.'

'Alright. Thanks for the offer anyway.'

He phoned Alison next.

'Hi Barney. What's up?'

He repeated exactly what he'd said to Liam.

But she responded with, 'No thanks. I hate swimming. Unless it's on a tropical beach.'

'Right, well I'll just bin it then.'

'It would be a shame to waste it. Why don't you use it yourself? You might enjoy it.'

'Nah. I probably wouldn't.'

'Give it a go. You've got nothing to lose. You might find it relaxing. Get rid of some of your stress.'

'Okay. We'll see.'

He didn't mean that when he was saying it, but after they ended the call, he was starting to think it might be worth giving it a try.

He was certainly going to have plenty of that stress Alison mentioned. He was about to be faced with one of those people he would like to kill. He was sent to a staff canteen where the manager had reported having trouble with her till. He'd been there several times before, and she had never had a kind word for him. He was always relieved to get the job finished and get out of there.

As usual she gave him a less than warm welcome. It may have been 'good afternoon', but to Barney it only sounded like some sort of grunt. Nevertheless, he stuck by his principles and approached things in a calm and pleasant manner.

'Hi, I hear you've been having problems with your till?'

'Have you brought the cable?'

'What cable?'

'I told them on the phone. I need a new cable. There's no point in you coming here if you haven't brought the cable. They should have told you that. Do people at your company not talk to each other?'

'Yes, but our policy is to send an engineer first to analyse the fault and decide what is needed, if anything. Spare parts can be very expensive and we don't want to buy parts which might not be needed.'

The woman was not going to be easily placated.

'Well take it from me, this part is definitely needed.'

'Do you mind if I take a look?'

Barney started walking towards the machine, but was stopped in his tracks.

'No, there's no point in touching the till if you've not got a cable.'

Barney looked at the till from a distance.

'Do you by any chance think it needs a new cable because the till is not communicating with the card reader?'

'That's right,' she said, in a most condescending tone. 'Now you're getting it.'

Barney enjoyed his next line, which he delivered with a quiet dignity.

'The till is not communicating with the card reader because you've plugged the cable into the wrong socket.'

'What?'

'There are two identical sockets for the cable. You've plugged it into the left one. If you plug it into the one on the right it should work.'

The woman realised she'd made a mistake, but wasn't the sort who could ever admit to being wrong.

'No, that isn't true. I've tried plugging it into both sockets. It still doesn't work.'

'Do you mind if I try it?'

'Yes, I do mind. Go away and come back with a new cable.'

'I will happily go away. But I won't be getting you a new cable.'

'So, you're saying you won't bring me a new cable?'

Out of Order

'Now you're getting it.'

Barney left, knowing fine well that as soon as he was out of sight, she would plug the cable into the correct socket and her till would miraculously start working.

Driving away, he considered whether it could be time to look for another job. He was sick of these people and was having a really difficult week. He imagined how better it would make him feel if the company occasionally showed a bit of gratitude. How nice it would be to receive the occasional Email from his boss along the lines of 'We know you've done a lot of difficult jobs this week and we really appreciate it. Keep up the good work. Many thanks for all your efforts.'

He was feeling so wound up that he decided Alison was right when she said he had nothing to lose by taking advantage of that free offer. So, he stopped off at home to quickly get changed. He didn't even own any kind of swimming gear, but he found an old pair of football shorts in the back of a drawer. They were a bit flimsy and had a couple of holes in them, and he would have to be careful none of his parts peeped out, but they would have to do. He shoved them in a plastic carrier bag and drove off to the leisure centre.

He handed his voucher to the receptionist and headed into the men's changing room. The first thing he noticed was the only one with a supermarket carrier bag. Everyone else had expensive looking sports bags.

He got changed into his shorts, which seemed even more flimsy when he was wearing them, and headed to the pool, beginning to regret coming.

Fortunately, there weren't many people in there. There was no way he was going to jump in, so he slowly worked his way down the steps into the water. He found it colder than he imagined. He just about remembered how to do the breaststroke, so did a couple of lengths. He was feeling self-conscious, thinking everyone else was watching him. He was also feeling cold, and decided to do something warmer.

He spotted a hot tub which looked quite inviting. But there was a man in it, talking on a mobile phone. This didn't help with Barney's de-stressing. It only wound him up even more. What kind of moron would want to take his phone with him into a jacuzzi? Talking in an unnecessarily loud voice too. He still wanted to go in though.

Even though it looked big enough for a few people, he wasn't sure what the etiquette was in these places. Could he just go in, or did he have to ask the occupant's permission? Or did he have to wait until the occupant came out before he went in?

He felt it would be awkward whichever option he chose, so instead he headed for the sauna. He sat down among a few people who were sitting there in silence. He found it all a bit weird, not to mention too hot. It would have been embarrassing to leave straight away, so he endured it for a few minutes, then got up and left. Luckily, he timed it perfectly. The man with the phone was just vacating the hot tub.

Out of Order

He climbed into the hot tub. That was much more to his liking. It was hot, but more bearable than the sauna. The bubbles were massaging him, and he started to relax.

After 15 minutes he was getting too hot and feeling a bit light headed, so decided it was time to get out. But just as he was about to leave, a young woman approached walked towards him and said, 'Do you mind if I join you?'

At least that answered his question about the etiquette.

'Not at all,' he managed to splutter.

He couldn't help but have a sneaky look at her dark, slender body before she sunk into the water. She was absolutely gorgeous. This was an unexpected bonus. Maybe his luck was changing for the better again. Then she started talking to him in an Indian accent.

She was friendly, and very chatty and he was enjoying her company even though the conversation wasn't exactly riveting. He was feeling uncomfortable hot by now, and a bit dizzy, but was reluctant to get out while he had the attention of such a beautiful woman.

After ten minutes she spoilt the moment by mentioning her husband. So, he decided this would be a good time to say goodbye and head for the exit. They had a bar in the leisure centre, and a cold pint of lager would be a much more reliable way of easing his stress.

But as usual, his plans went awry when something else popped up. Literally! And had found its way out through one of the holes in his shorts. Fortunately for him, and for anyone else nearby, the bubbles in the hot tub were preventing anyone from seeing what was going on down there. He tried to maintain his dignity and keep the conversation going, while fumbling around under the water trying to put things back in order. He was unsure if the young lady was aware of what she had induced, but a slight mischievous grin suggested that she was.

He managed, to an extent, to put things right, at least as far as getting back through the hole was concerned. But he still couldn't get out yet. Not in these woefully inadequate shorts, which weren't going to hide his embarrassment. He would have to endure the heat for a bit longer.

It became more than just a bit. She stayed in the tub for another 10 minutes and was still making small talk, but by now he wasn't listening, and was just nodding and saying yes. The warmth of the water wasn't helping his problem subside. He was feeling horribly uncomfortable, and becoming quite nauseous. It came as a big relief when she finally said goodbye, stood up and climbed out. Watching her from behind going up the steps was not going to do much to ease his difficulty, and only served to prolong his stay.

He'd now been in the jacuzzi, which he was beginning to hate, for 40 minutes, and couldn't stand it for a moment longer. So when he thought nobody was watching, he took a gamble and he hurried up the steps and jumped straight into the pool. Once he was in there, the combination of the cold water and the absence of the Indian lady soon had him shrivelled up again, so he got out and went to get changed.

In the changing room he took his clothes out of the locker and attempted to dry himself. An attempt which would have been made a whole lot easier if it had occurred to him to bring a towel.

He walked out into the cold air with his clothes still damp, because he'd had to put them on while he was still wet, feeling that his visit hadn't had the desired outcome. He didn't feel like going into the bar while he was damp, so he went straight home. He was more stressed than ever.

He parked his car outside his house and his phone pinged. He had indeed received an Email from work. Could they really be sending him a thank you for all his hard work? But it wasn't from his boss. It was from the fleet department.

'We have been checking your petrol receipts and have seen that on one occasion recently you filled up your car with premium petrol instead of standard fuel. This has resulted in a bill which is £2.34 higher than it should have been. May I remind you that this is against company policy. Any repeat of this and we will have to report this to your line manager and disciplinary action may be taken against you.'

Barney briefly contemplated writing a reply telling them what he thought of them, but he didn't have the required mental strength at this moment. He just went into the house and plopped down on the sofa. Then his phone rang. It was his mum. What she had to say offered him a chance of a short escape from his troubles.

21

The lake district was a pleasant place to visit at any time of the year, but autumn was Barney's favourite. It was usually warm enough without being too hot. There were still plenty of tourists around, but not the crowds that come in the summer months. The scenery was even better than usual due to the leaves on the trees changing colour.

On his last few visits there he had been doing something called 'Tarn Dipping'. The idea was to visit all 197 tarns, or mountain lakes, and dip your hand into them. Or indeed any part of you. Up to now he had managed to tick off 68 of them, so he still had a long way to go. It was basically just an excuse to visit beautiful places. A bit like when some of the lads in the darts team went to pubs, just to tick them off from their CAMRA book.

Best of all was the added bonus of having somewhere to stay for free. Barney's mum ran a B&B which was always fully booked during the summer, but sometimes on weekends in the autumn or early spring, there would be an empty room. When that happened, Barney's mum would call him two or three days in advance and he would knock off work at noon on Friday and go there for the weekend.

This week she had called him on Wednesday saying there had been a cancellation. He was pleased to hear it. It was a haven. He could escape from the stress of work, and more importantly he could escape from people. His mum was usually busy with the B&B, so he had most of the time to himself. That was the way he preferred it. It was good to see her, but he could only take so much of her before she started driving him mad. She treated him like he was still a naughty ten-year-old at times. So, when he could escape, he would go for long walks in the countryside, or sit by a lake and chill out. There were plenty of good pubs around, and he liked to pop in for lunch either in one of his favourites, or exploring new ones. Then there was the pub in the village which even had a dartboard, where he would go on a Saturday evening for a game of darts and a couple of pints.

The downside, as is often the case when visiting someone in Britain, was the journey. If he didn't get away from work early enough on Friday, the traffic on the M6 just north of Birmingham could be hell.

Today wasn't too bad. He had hit the M40 just before one o'clock, and was well past Birmingham before the heavy traffic built up. Unfortunately, he had to drive past Junction 21A on the M6 and the sign to Liverpool, and had a painful reminder of his exploits last Thursday.

He arrived in the lake district early enough to spend some time with his mum, and still have time to pop out for a pint.

His mum had cooked him what she thought was one of his favourite meals, even though it wasn't particularly, although it was nice enough. She told him all of her latest news, and he told her some, but not all of his latest news. But he was getting restless, so told her, 'Right, I think I'll pop out for a walk. Stretch my legs after my long journey.'

'OK. What time will you be back?'

'I don't know. Does it matter? Don't wait up for me. I've got a key.'

'You're not going out without a jacket, are you?'

'Mum. I'm 45 years old. I can make my own mind up about wearing a jacket.'

'You'll catch your death of cold.'

'No, I won't. You don't die from having a cold. And the only people who catch a cold from actually being cold are characters in comics or bad sitcoms who fall into rivers, or get stuck inside the fridge. Anyway, it's quite warm out there. And It only takes five minutes to get to the pub.'

'I thought you said you were going for a walk.'

'I am. I'm going for a walk to the pub.'

He managed to get out to the pub by nine o'clock.

The village pub was called the Fisherman's Retreat, but none of the clientele looked like fishermen. Although he'd been there before several times, he hadn't got to know anyone, apart from the bar staff, and recognised the odd familiar face. It was in a location where a lot of tourists would come and go. He sometimes had a game of darts with visitors or locals, but tonight the darts area was unusually busy, with a crowd of people taking turns throwing at the board.

Barney watched them for a while and got talking to a woman called Sue. He had learnt a harsh lesson in Torquay, and was determined never to make the same mistake again. From now on he would always ask their name and commit it to memory. Sue explained to him they were having a charity dartathon. A group of about twelve people were throwing darts for 24 hours to raise money for the BBC Children in Need appeal. Barney made a small donation and Sue invited him to join in. So, he got his darts out and had a few throws.

She explained to him they had started at six o'clock, and were planning on going through the night and all through Saturday until six o'clock came around again. Barney and Sue continued chatting and drinking, and in the blink of an eye it was midnight. Barney was getting on exceptionally well with Sue. She didn't appear to be with any of the men in the group and Barney thought yet again his luck might have changed. He wasn't optimistic about lasting all night playing darts, but he was determined to hang on as long as he possibly could to see how things developed. But as usual when all was going well, there was a giant spanner around the corner that was about to be put in the works.

Just after one o'clock two policemen in uniform walked in and went up to the bar. They didn't appear to be on official business, and this was confirmed when the barman poured them a pint each. On the house. The two policemen took their time over their drinks, then one of them wandered over to the darts area.

'Is one of you called Cecil Barnard?' He asked in a typical policeman's tone from the 1960s, or 70s. A mixture of over politeness and sarcasm. The only thing that was missing was 'evening all'. Or 'hello, hello, hello'.

Barney was shocked and instantly worried.

'Yes, that's me. What's wrong?'

'Mrs. Barnard called me. She's a good friend of mine. She wanted to report you missing.'

'You can't be serious. I only left her at nine o'clock. I'm not missing.'

'I know that, sir. I told her you couldn't be officially missing after only three and a half hours. But I promised her I would keep an eye out for you.'

Barney couldn't believe it.

'I told her where I was going.'

'She expected you home before now.'

'It's not my home. I live two hundred and seventy miles from here. And I'm forty-five years old. Not twelve. Why couldn't she have just phoned me instead?'

'I don't know that sir. But perhaps you best be getting along now. As I just said, your mum is a good friend of mine and I wouldn't want to see her unduly worried.'

Barney didn't want to leave. And the police didn't have the power to make him leave. He could probably have threatened to report the policeman for drinking in a pub while he was still in uniform, but he didn't even know if that was against the rules, and the other problem could be that if he really was a friend of his mums, he didn't want to do something that might upset her. He wasn't as good at arguing with policemen as he was with vending machine users. And some of the other darts players were looking at him as if he was a heartless monster, treating his poor mum in such an inconsiderate way.

He didn't appear to have much choice. He reluctantly left the pub, and even more reluctantly left Sue.

He mumbled and cursed his way back to the B&B. He was forty-five years old and his mum was still telling him what time he had to be home. But he couldn't face an argument with her at this hour. Or any hour. He could never win any argument against her. She had a crazy logic which drove him nuts. She was still awake and relieved to see him, so he gave a brief explanation of where he'd been and went to bed. On his own. Yet again.

He wanted to go back to the pub on Saturday afternoon and rejoin the dartathon and more importantly, Sue, but his mum had booked them on a boat trip which he could hardly say no to. It was pleasant enough. He normally liked being on water, and his mum knew it. That's why she booked the excursion. But he struggled to show his appreciation. She had unwittingly dealt another blow to his faltering love life for the second day running. The boat trip was quite a long drive from the village. By the time they'd got back to the B&B it was seven o'clock. He dashed to the Fisherman's Retreat, but the dartathon was over and they had all gone home. Including Sue.

He sat in the pub for a while, but thought it would be wise to go back to his mum's place earlier than he would have normally done in case her 'good friend' Dixon of Dock Green came by again.

On Sunday morning he went for a walk in one of his favourite spots. It was a huge open space on high ground with breathtaking views for miles with lakes and trees, and very few people to be seen. He would usually spend a few hours there. But this time it wasn't working its magic spell. He was getting little satisfaction from it. He hadn't even managed to tick off any new tarn dips. The weekend had not provided the relaxation therapy he needed, so he headed back south earlier than planned.

22

It was Monday morning, and the beginning of the week when Alison was going for her hospital appointment. The heart attack had been a distraction, but she was back in full worry mode now. No matter how hard she tried, she couldn't think of anything else. But the cocktail of drugs she had been given at the hospital were hopefully preventing her from coming to any more harm as far as her heart was concerned.

At least she would know what the problem was very soon. She had two more days of work to get through first. Her first call of the morning was at Slough Crematorium, refilling a snack machine. Although the customer was officially listed on the call as Slough Crematorium the machine was located in the cemetery. They had a snack machine and coffee dispenser in the workers hut in the middle of a large graveyard. She'd been there a few times before, but usually later in the day. This time it was seven o'clock in the morning in November and it was still dark. This only occurred to her as she got out her van. She would have to walk in the dark through a graveyard. No way! It's not that she believed in ghosts. Nor did she think there'd be any graverobbers lurking around who would happily murder anyone who discovered them. She just didn't fancy it much.

She jumped back into the van and planned her next move. Maybe Barney was in the vicinity. He might be prepared to come with her.

She called his number, but immediately felt silly. Even before he answered, she decided not to mention the cemetery.

Feeling silly had been unnecessary. Barney would have been a lot more sympathetic than she imagined. Many years ago, when he was working for Hot Cup, he was sent to do a job in the London Dungeon. It was before opening time, so there were no members of the public in yet. He was left on his own to repair their machine surrounded by grisly exhibits. The only people around were members of staff wearing gruesome costumes, which didn't help at all. He was really freaked out by it and almost ran out at one point. So, he would understand her reluctance to walk among gravestones in the dark.

'Hi Barney. I was just calling to check that you were still coming with me on Wednesday?'

'Yes. You keep asking me, and I keep telling you. I'll be there. I know it's difficult, but try to stop worrying.'

'OK. Thanks. How was Torquay?'

'Very boring. The others on the course were just a typical bunch of nerds. The hotel was nice enough though. I had a couple of pints in a pub on Thursday evening, but that was about as exciting as it got.'

There was no way he wanted to tell her about what happened after the pub with Attractive Scouse Vendetta Woman (he still didn't know her name). He didn't want to tell anybody. Once the Vendetta grapevine went into full swing, everyone in the office, plus the ones out on the road would know. He'd be ridiculed mercilessly.

'And how was the Lake District?'

'I've had better visits.'

'OK then. What about your free spa trip to the leisure centre?'

Barney just let out a huge sigh. Alison knew it was time to stop asking questions.

They continued to chat for a while and it had just started to get light. After they ended the call, she sat for another ten minutes and decided it was light enough and she was brave enough to walk past the gravestones to carry out her work.

Alison detected something strange about the phone call with Barney. She didn't know why, but she had a feeling there were things he wasn't telling her. But even if he was, it wasn't any of her business anyway. So why was it bothering her so much?

The rest of her day went without any troubles. She was filling up a canned drink machine when a man came up to her and said, 'Can you put some whisky in there?' and chuckled with satisfaction. She hated it when people said that. Oh, how much she wanted to say, 'I've never heard that one before. You are so original. Has anyone ever told you how funny you are? Or do they tend to tell you to shut the fuck up and go away?'

But she resisted the temptation. Her irritation was soon to be replaced with a moment of supreme satisfaction.

She was dealing with a trio of vending machines in the library of Brunel University, just outside Uxbridge.

There was a hot drinks machine, a snack machine, and a bottles and cans machine. She had just finished filling them when a young student bought a can of Coke from the cold drinks machine. He started yelling and hurling abuse at the machine, although she knew it was aimed at her really, because it wouldn't give him his change. Customers such as this were the ones she disliked most. The ones who aimed spiteful comments at her, but did it as if she wasn't in the room.

When she was a kid, libraries were silent places, and someone would shush you if you made the tiniest sound. Things seem to be a bit more relaxed these days and there was a low level of chatter around the place. But it wasn't enough to block out the noise this idiot was making with his shouting and swearing. She walked up to the machine slowly and coolly without saying a word, pressed the button marked "Return Change" and walked away slowly and coolly as his 15p dropped loudly into the coin return compartment. She glanced back briefly just to check his embarrassment, of which there was plenty. Everyone was looking at him. A most satisfying moment indeed. Was this moron an example of the educated section of our society? He'd no doubt get his degree and end up as a manager like Richard Bowles.

She was desperate to tell Barney about it. He would enjoy it as much as she had. But she didn't. She couldn't keep calling him. She'll keep it for later.

Coincidentally, Barney was less than a mile way. He had gone to Uxbridge town centre to help Liam with a job he was having a bit of difficulty completing. It didn't take him too long. Liam often struggled when the answer was simple. He tended to look for more complicated solutions, when all that was required was a bit of logical thinking.

As usual when they got together for a job, they popped into a pub for some refreshments. It rarely turned into a big session, mainly because they both had cars with them and would have to drive home. It was really just an excuse to catch up on some old gossip, or start some new gossip, and to slag off the management. Which they did. Liam normally bought food, as he was always hungry, but the pub had stopped serving lunch by this time. Barney was hungry too, so he suggested they went next door to a fried chicken restaurant. Liam didn't need to think long about it. A bucket of chicken was just what he needed.

It prompted Barney to ask, 'How can you have a go at me for eating bacon sandwiches, yet you've happy to eat a bucket full of fried chicken and chips?'

'Ah but I don't have it every day. I'm only doing it to keep you company.'

'Rubbish. You're always eating. Hypocrite.'

Liam, as he usually did, took the comments to heart and went in a huff.

Apart from the two of them there was only one other person in the restaurant. Sitting on the table next to them was a rather large elderly lady. There was a bench which ran the length of the two tables. Barney was on the same bench as the lady. As they ate their food, she let out a thunderous fart which was so ferocious Barney was sure he felt the bench shudder. To her credit, instead of pretending it didn't happen, she mumbled an embarrassed apology.

For the duration of his attempt to enjoy his spicy wings and chips, she repeated the trick at regular intervals. She must have been approaching double figures by the time they finished. Once again Barney had to go through the agony of not laughing. He could never understand why the British found farting so hilarious. It was just a natural bodily function. Nobody laughs at a sneeze or a burp. Despite that he found this particular situation funny, and it was made even more difficult because Liam was trying not to laugh too. But they did manage to keep it together and spared the poor woman's blushes.

As they parted Liam thanked Barney for his help.

Barney said, 'That's OK. You can return the favour on Tuesday next week. I've got to install a large food machine in an office canteen on the outskirts of Maidenhead. I have to wheel the machine in on a pump truck and we're not allowed to do it with less than two people.'

'No bother. Send me a copy of the job, so I've got the where and when.'

They went their separate ways, Barney had one more call to make. It was somewhere he'd never been before. It was at a riding stable somewhere in the Buckinghamshire countryside.

Out of Order

His mission was to repair an ice cream cabinet.

Although the journey took him through some very pleasant countryside, the drive wasn't quite so pleasant. He had to drive the final two miles on a single-track road with passing places. He was forced to reverse three times to let oncoming vehicles past. He wondered why it was always him reversing and never the other car. He eventually got there in one piece.

It was an unusual place to work because he was used to bustling offices and noisy factories, but this place was silent apart from a background of animal noises. There were two or three staff around, cleaning stables and feeding horses, and more importantly leaving him alone to get on with his work.

He was progressing nicely and was in deep concentration when he felt a nudge on his neck. When he turned to see who it was, he found himself face to face with a horse. The horse kept nudging him and he thought it was about to bite him. He ended up running away with the horse in hot pursuit. He managed to duck inside a building and close the door. One of the staff eventually found him and led the horse away, allowing him to return to the ice cream cabinet, which he duly got up and running.

He doubted the others would believe him when told this tale. At least the horse wouldn't be phoning to make a complaint about him.

23

It was promising to be an eventful week ahead for Barney. On Wednesday he was accompanying Alison to the hospital. She had been dreading it for weeks. Now he was getting a bit nervous himself. He wasn't very confident of being much use to her if it didn't go well. But she was relying on him, so he would try his best.

On Thursday there was the last darts match of the year to look forward to. That was always a big occasion, and a very big drink.

But first he had to get through a bit more work. He could do with an easy few days. But his customer relation skills were about to be put to the test again.

It was that old 'health and safety' chestnut that was to cause him grief today. He wasn't belittling the importance of health and safety. In theory it was a good thing. He'd had his fair share of accidents over the years to realise that. Also, he once again remembered years ago hearing someone say twice as many people were killed by vending machines on average every year than there were killed by sharks. And he wouldn't be reckless enough to dive headlong into shark infested waters. But sometimes it went way over the top. He was often forced to waste time watching videos and filling in forms, when all that was really needed was for people to just act with a bit of common sense. Then of course there were too many people around who didn't have any.

Out of Order

An example of this was a job he did fairly recently where he was working on a refrigeration unit which was at the bottom of a vending machine, and to reach the component he was working on, he had to lie on the floor. It was in a small kitchen, and the site contact had put a barrier across the doorway which was marked 'Danger. Do Not Enter'. Because he was lying on the ground measuring live voltages, he was happy on this occasion for them to take his safety seriously. But while he was working, a woman ducked under the barrier, stepped over him, and stood on his open case full of sharp tools to press a button on the vending machine which had the door open, and a large 'out of order' sign stuck to it. No doubt he would have got the blame if she'd tripped over him and scalded herself, or a chisel had chopped her toe off.

He was sent to a huge factory in Hayes, and the reported fault looked simple enough. Hot chocolate not dispensing. That shouldn't take too long.

On arrival he was met by a young man who wouldn't have been born when Barney first started working. He started going through the company's health and safety policy. He started off by asking Barney if he was 'competent' to do the job and could he sign the Risk Assessment and Method Statement form to confirm this.

Barney was in an impatient mood and was unnecessarily sarcastic. 'I must admit, I've had the odd electric shock, and cut myself a few times. I've caused a couple of smoke alarms to go off, I've scalded myself on a regular basis, and I've tripped over on more than one occasion. In fact, you could say I'm a walking disaster area. But to answer your question, I would say yes I am competent.'

The young man didn't react to any of that. Instead, he just ticked the box marked 'Yes'.

'Are you qualified?'

'I did Electrical and Electronic Engineering at a University in London. I passed. Will that suffice?'

'Do you have a certificate?'

'Not with me. I stopped carrying it around twenty years ago. I was worried I might spill blood on it.'

'I'd better tick no for that one then. Who is at risk from the work you're doing today? Choices are, yourself, colleagues, general public, or young people.'

'Young people?'

The young man ticked the box marked young people.

Barney said, 'No, no, that wasn't my choice. I was questioning it. What do you mean by young people?'

'Well, I suppose it might mean small children for instance.'

'Are there any small children in the factory?'

'No.'

'In that case shall we assume I'm no danger to them?'

'OK.'

'I have no colleagues with me. Can we scratch that one too?'

'I suppose so.'

'General public? Do people wander in and out from the street on a regular basis?'

'No.'

'That just leaves myself. I would say that I am putting myself at risk, because I'm going to be worn out and in danger of falling asleep on the job by the time you let me start.'

The young man ticked the box marked 'Yourself'.

'What precautions will you put in place to ensure the safety of the people at risk?'

'I don't know.'

'I have to put something down.'

'I really don't know. Can't you just make something up?'

'I'm only following the regulations. My job requires me to ask these things.'

Eventually they got through the form and he was allowed to go to the machine. The young man had to escort him and watch him do the job, which consisted of unblocking and cleaning a pipe which the hot chocolate flowed down, and it took him about two minutes. He came to no harm. He then had to sign yet more paperwork saying he had completed the work and left the equipment in a safe condition.

After leaving the building, he felt a touch of guilt. Perhaps he shouldn't have been so stroppy. The young lad was only doing his job after all and probably thought the whole thing was as much a waste of time as he did.

He sailed through the rest of the day, and his last job was the one he liked best. It was changing a light tube in a machine. It was the easiest of tasks, and the only downside was the prospect of having to take the old tube to the recycling centre.

He had been to this particular site before. As recently as two weeks ago. It was an office full of women, who were all very loud and thought they were funny. On that visit two weeks ago, he had been dispatched there because their snack machine was too dark to see the products.

He had informed them, 'The light bulb has blown.'

One of the women responded with 'Ooh. Stop trying to baffle us with science. We're just simple women. Give it to us in plain English.'

'It needs a new bulb.'

'Gasp! That is amazing. You are so clever. For a man.'

The other women enjoyed that and cackled loudly.

'Yeah, very funny, said Barney. 'I'll get you a new one and will return as soon as possible.'

One of the women asked, 'How long do you think it will be?'

Barney stretched out his arms as if he was describing how big a fish he had caught and said, 'About this long.'

'Now who's being funny?'

'I'm doing you a favour anyway. If you can't see what's in the machine you will be less tempted to buy anything. Some of you look like you've been eating too many chocolates and crisps lately.'

One of them threw something at him as he was going out of the door. Luckily it missed.

It wouldn't normally take two weeks for a spare part to be delivered. He didn't know why it had taken so long this time. But he marched into the office triumphantly waving the fluorescent light tube above his head. The women in the office all applauded and cheered. But this turned to raucous laughter when he tripped over a step in the doorway and the tube smashed to pieces on the floor.

He lay sprawled out on the floor for a while hoping that some of them would have a bit of sympathy and help him up. But no. One of them, still laughing, brought him a dustpan and sweeping brush.

He got to his feet and swept up the broken glass, then tried his best to disguise his embarrassment. He said, 'Just to let you know, your machine needs a new light bulb. I'll get one and return as soon as possible,' then tried to sneak out of the door.

There were a few things shouted at him as he was leaving, accompanied with more laughter.

'OK. See you in two weeks.'

'How many Vendetta engineers does it take to change a light bulb?'

'Just the one. But it takes him four weeks and he nearly kills himself doing it.'

'Would you like us to get a 'Mind the Step' sign before you come back?'

He was relieved to escape. But was proud of the service he had provided. Giving them all such a good laugh was far more beneficial for them than the chocolates and crisps would have been. He would no doubt have to face more ridicule when he returned, which he didn't relish much, so he came up with a sneaky idea. He phoned Liam.

'Alright Barney?'

'Alright Liam? Do you have any flo tubes in your car? I urgently need one.'

'Yeah, I've got some. I can bring one to you if you want?'

'Well, I was thinking it would be easier if you just go and fit it. I can call Mary and get her to transfer the job to you?'

'Yeah, no bother.'

'Cheers.'

Barney didn't feel the slightest bit guilty for his deviousness. OK, Liam might get laughed at, but he would have an easy job to his name. And he would love the attention he would get from all of those women. They would no doubt treat him nicer anyway, because he was taller and better looking than Barney was.

Another thing occurred to him as he drove away. If this was embarrassing, just imagine how it would feel if it had happened at a job such as the one this morning after he'd been making such a fuss about their health and safety procedure.

24

As Barney had mentioned to Liam the previous week, he needed his help on a job today. He was installing a food machine in the office canteen of a pharmaceutical giant. Normally the logistics department who delivered the machines would put them in position and all the engineer would have to do was put the plug in, do a bit of programming, and connect the water supply in the case of coffee machines, then test them to make sure they were functioning properly.

Usually, it was the most straightforward of jobs. But today was going to be different. Barney had been tipped off by Mary that the machine wasn't in situ. He would have to move it. That was why he'd invited Liam along. He might need some muscle power.

Barney and Liam met in the car park and walked to the reception. The canteen was run by an independent catering company, and the canteen manager came to the reception to greet them. He introduced himself as Martin. He already looked like he was having a stressful day. Then he led them to the vending machine, which was standing in a corridor next to a lift.

Martin started to explain.

'We need to get the machine up to the restaurant which is on the second floor. It's essential we get this done today.'

Liam let Barney do the talking.

'Why isn't it already in the restaurant?'

'The people who delivered it said it wouldn't fit in the lift. So, they refused to take in any further and left.'

Barney acted confused. 'But if they couldn't get it into the lift, what makes you think we'll be able to?'

'They didn't even try. They measured the machine and the lift door, then said it would be a waste of time even trying. But I measured it myself and I'm sure it will go in,' he replied. But he didn't sound so sure. He sounded as if he was trying to convince himself.

Barney got the impression the manager was under pressure to get this machine up and running, and was acting out of desperation. The logistics department could be difficult at times. He'd had to deal with them several times, including the recent fiasco with Laurel and Hardy at the Heathrow Airport hotel. But they were also experienced in moving vending machines in and out of lifts. He was leaning toward believing them rather than Martin. The only way to be certain was to check for himself.

He took the tape measure out of his tool bag and measured the lift doors. He didn't need to measure the machine. He already knew its dimensions. He turned to Martin.

'I think they might have a point. It's very tight. We're talking millimetres here.'

Martin started to get agitated.

'We have another machine exactly the same as this one already up there. It must have gone up in this lift.'

Out of Order

'OK. Well give it a try. But we'll need a pump truck.'

Martin disappeared, then returned ten minutes later with a pump truck which Barney thought looked too small for the task. They pushed the truck under the machine and tried to raise it. The machine started to wobble and Barney had seen enough.

'I'm not happy with this. It's too dangerous.'

Martin was fuming by now. But he couldn't really argue. Deep down he knew Barney was correct. He made a phone call and three men soon appeared. They looked rather clueless and didn't inspire confidence.

'If you're not willing to move it, we'll just have to move it ourselves.' said Martin.

Barney and Liam moved out of the way and left them to it. They couldn't leave because they still had to get the machine working if it ever made it to its final destination, so all they could do for now was stand back and watch.

It made for interesting watching too. Barney and Liam decided it was like watching the real Laurel and Hardy trying to carry a piano up some stairs, or watching 'Carry On Vending' starring Kenneth Williams as Martin and Sid James as Barney. Liam asked what time Barbara Windsor was turning up.

'Given my recent luck with women, it would more likely be Hattie Jacques,' Barney told him.

The huge machine lurched around on the woefully inadequate pump truck while these four clowns manhandled it towards the lift door.

In the end they did actually get it into the lift, but not without a few crashes and bangs and bits and pieces flying everywhere. The lift door had taken a hit too. By the time it had eventually been set down in its location it had been damaged too badly for them to get it working.

Barney explained to Martin, who had completely lost his cool by now, that he would need to order some parts and return. There would also be the small matter of who was going to pay for the replacement parts and labour. He didn't believe acts of stupidity were included in the service contract. But that was Richard Bowles's problem.

He and Liam made their escape, then did what had become traditional when they'd done a job together. They went into the nearest pub for a pint and discussed what had just happened. Barney told Liam a tale from his early days in the job at Hot Cup when he spilled descaling acid on someone's jacket and ended up having to pay for it, even though it was the jacket owner's fault. His point was if he'd been more experienced, he would have refused to do the job, so today they made the right call in refusing to move the machine. It was one of those tricky situations that could have backfired on them. If Martin and the three stooges had managed to get the machine up to the canteen in one piece, Barney would have been portrayed as the trouble causer yet again, refusing to do the job he was paid to do. But if he and Liam had tried to move it and caused the damage that happened, they would be in bigger trouble.

Barney said to Liam, 'You might have to cover some of my calls tomorrow. I'm taking the afternoon off.'

Out of Order

'I thought you took every afternoon off.'

'Very funny. And that's only partially true.'

'So why are you taking the afternoon off?'

'I'm going with Alison to the hospital. She's got an eye test and is extremely worried about it. Also, she has to have someone with her to drive her home and has nobody else to do it.'

'Oh, that doesn't sound good. Is it serious then?'

'It could be. She's been looking up stuff on the Internet and has seen photos and articles about glaucoma. She's fearing the worst. I'm not exactly looking forward to it myself.'

They finished their drinks and Liam headed for home.

Barney had time to squeeze one more job in before he packed up for the day. It was in Slough Town centre, so it was near to home. He drove to Slough, and struggled to find a parking space. He was lucky enough to find an empty bay in the second place off the end of a block of parking bays and paid for a ticket. There were always parking enforcement officers, although Barney still referred to them as traffic wardens, around these streets. If he was a few minutes late he would expect a penalty charge notice to be stuck on his windscreen. But there was no chance of that today. The job was easy and he was done in twenty minutes. But when he got back to his car, the car that had been parked on the end bay had gone and was replaced by another one, which was parked across the line and into his bay, right up to the bumper. There was no way Barney could get his car out. He grabbed the attention of a traffic warden.

'Excuse me. Can you give this moron a penalty charge please?'

'Why?'

'Look where he's parked. I can't get out.'

'No. I can't.'

'Why not?'

'I decide who gets parking fines. Not you.'

Then he walked off. Barney was furious. If the driver had returned at that point, he would have thumped him. He would have liked to hit the traffic warden too. It was the first time he actually wanted one of them to give out a ticket and he refused.

Having no idea how long he was going to be there, he got in the car and started the engine. Then he pushed his car against the other one and found it moved quite easily. So, he pushed it until he thought there was enough space to get his car out. He got out and had a look at how much space he'd created. The end of the other car had been pushed over the end of the bay. Barney thought it would serve him right if he was given a fine by an overzealous traffic warden. Then he thought, 'if you're going to do something, you might as well do it properly.'

He got back in his car and waited until there was nobody around. Then he revved up his engine and pushed the other car completely out of the bay onto a double yellow line.

'Now, Mister parking attendant officer. Do your stuff.'

He drove away, but then became curious to know if his plan had worked. So, he parked his car in the next street, walked back and sat outside a pub where he had a clear view of the car. After ten

Out of Order

minutes a different traffic warden put a penalty charge notice onto the car windscreen. Barney was delighted. He was about to leave, but now he wanted to watch for the victim's reaction. It took forty minutes and two pints, but it was worth it. A man came back to the car and saw the notice. He looked at his watch puzzled. Then he read the notice. He walked around his car a few times, wondering why he was parked on yellow lines. He chased after a parking enforcement officer and hurled abuse at him. Barney sat watching, drinking his beer, thoroughly enjoying himself, and pleased with his efforts. He didn't think he was a vindictive person, but he certainly enjoyed watching people get their comeuppance.

25

Although her appointment wasn't until mid-afternoon, Alison had been given the whole day off by her supervisor. She thought that was decent of her, but didn't feel the need to be off all day. Barney didn't ask for any time off. He would go to work in the morning and finish when it suited him. He was doing them a favour by looking after one of their employees. She had been told not to drive to the hospital because some of the tests would leave her with blurry vision for a while. So he would have to drive her there and home again.

But as she sat around at home, waiting, watching the clock, she thought she would have been better off going to work, to take her mind off things.

Although he saved time by sacrificing his regular bacon sandwich, Barney had an easy morning. But he did get asked an unusual question while he was in the middle of a job. He was sorting out someone's coffee machine when a woman came up to him and said, 'Do you know much about the supernatural?'

Barney couldn't tell if she was being serious.

'Errm... not a great lot. My field of expertise tends to be vending machines. And a bit of cricket. Darts perhaps. The Simpsons. Tarn dipping.'

The woman appeared to take no notice of his answer and continued. 'I've just received a message from another dimension and I don't know what it means.'

'I see,' said Barney, even though he didn't see at all. 'What was the message?'

But she didn't answer. She just wandered off. He never found out whether it was some sort of prank, or if she was just off her rocker. Or if indeed she had actually received a message from another dimension.

He finished the job and got out of there as quickly as he could.

He arrived at Alison's house in High Wycombe in good time and they set off. The hospital was in Aylesbury, and the journey took just over half an hour. Alison sat in silence so Barney thought she needed a distraction.

'Back in my days working for Hot Cup I was sent to Moorfields eye hospital in London. It's quite a funny tale.'

Alison wasn't in the mood for something funny.

'Oh yes. A joke about an eye hospital. That's just what I need.'

'It's not a joke. It's a true story. The receptionist wouldn't let me in because I had no contact name. Then I phoned our service desk, who were nowhere near as clued up as Mary. They told me to ask for Len. Which I did. But the reception didn't know anyone called Len. They looked through lists of names and made a few calls, but couldn't locate him. After half an hour I was becoming frustrated so I called the service desk again. I asked if they had a second name for Len. They said they hadn't. All they had was a note saying "Contact Lenses department". It was the only information they could give me. No phone number. At that point it became obvious why.'

Alison managed a small laugh.

'Did that really happen?'

'Yes. I swear. It really did.'

On arrival Barney put his car in the car park. This time he was definitely going to charge the company for the car park payment.

They entered the hospital and looked on the board for the eye department. When they found it, they were told to sit in the waiting area. They sat for quite a while, which didn't help Alison very much. He could see she was shaking. He felt terrible for her. There were quite a few other people waiting, but it was completely silent.

When her name was called out, she stood up and followed one of the staff into a small room where she was asked a few questions. Then she was taken into a bigger room full of the sort of machinery that she'd seen at the opticians. They carried out similar tests to the ones she'd done before. The cartoon chart with letters. The puff of air into the eyes. They repeated some of them. Then she was taken into another room with more equipment. There were yet more tests, slightly different to the ones she'd done before. One of these involved having something sprayed into her eyes. She had been warned about this. It was the reason she would have blurry vision for a while. She had also been advised to bring a pair of sunglasses to wear for a while when she came out.

After the testing was done, she was led into another room where a man coolly and calmly went through the results of her tests. She was aggrieved he could deliver the news in such a matter-of-fact manner. This was such a huge deal for her. Perhaps it was because he did this all day every day. But this was all about people's eyesight. She worked in a world where people got hysterical because their coffee was a bit weak. People had strange priorities. She listened as he went through the results. The beginning of each sentence gave her either a brief moment of optimism, or despair. Some of it was jargon she couldn't fully understand. But she was in no doubt what he meant when he delivered his final verdict.

Barney had wandered off for half an hour because he couldn't bear sitting around in that waiting room any longer. There wasn't anywhere to go. There were no pubs and no shops, so he wandered around aimlessly for half an hour. He was back in time to meet Alison as she walked back into the waiting area. There was no expression on her face. She was wearing sunglasses, but he could see tears running down her cheeks. This was just a side effect of the spray. Or so he hoped.

The only thing he could think of saying was an inadequate, 'How did it go?'

She tried to speak, but couldn't get any words out. He led her over to an area where there weren't any people. They stayed quiet for a while. He was giving her time to compose herself. Then although she was still struggling to string a sentence together, she eventually managed to tell him what had happened.

'I don't fully understand it, but they said something about me having thicker than usual corneas.'

'Oh. What does that mean? Is it serious?'

'They said it can cause false pressure readings at the opticians because their equipment is not as sophisticated as the stuff they've got at the hospital'

'So, what are they going to do next?'

'Nothing. They say my eyes are perfectly healthy.'

Then the real tears came. Mainly from Alison, but the situation was getting to Barney too. They hugged each other and stayed like that for a while. Eventually Barney said, 'Come on. Let's get you out of here.'

On the journey home they weren't any chattier than the journey there. She was just so overwhelmed with relief. So was he. When they arrived at her house, she invited him in for coffee. She was talking a lot more now, but mainly babbling about nothing in particular.

She made them coffee, and while they were drinking it, she said, 'I could do with something stronger.'

Barney relished the opportunity. He suggested, 'How would you like to go to the pub for a celebration drink?'

'Yes. I think that's a good idea. I'd like that.'

'But only if you promise not to talk about vending machines.'

'It's a deal.'

They waited a while until her eyes were clear and she didn't need the sunglasses. Then they went to a pub she used to go to years ago, but hadn't been in since her divorce.

'I've got another humorous tale about a job I did in a hospital if you want to hear it?'

'I thought you didn't want to talk about work?'

'No. I said I didn't want to talk about vending machines. Work related gossip and funny stories don't count.'

'Alright, let's hear it.'

'Have you ever been to Ealing hospital?'

'No. That's well away from my patch.'

'I went there for a job once, and reported to the main reception. The receptionist asked me if I knew the location of the machine as they had quite a few scattered around the hospital. I said I'd been told it was in the RSU. I didn't know what that was. She told me to drive up a hill to the far end of the hospital and check in with the reception next to the tall barbed wire fences. It wasn't like any reception I'd ever seen. They asked me lots of questions. Then they searched me. They also made me take all the sharp tools out of my tool case. It turns out RSU stood for Regional Secure Unit. A security guard had to escort me at all times. I could hear shouting and screaming while I was trying to work. It was very unnerving.'

Alison said, 'That's not an amusing tale.'

'No. I suppose it's more of a scary tale. Not as scary as a job I did in the London Dungeon. Or the time I had to walk through the graveyard at Slough Crematorium in the dark. That totally freaked me out. I even started running at one stage.'

Alison burst out laughing.

'I can't believe you were too scared to walk through a graveyard just because it was dark. What a wuss!'

She wasn't going to spoil the moment by telling him about her own experience in Slough Crematorium. Instead, she told him all about her eye tests. Then she told him all about her ex-husband. About how horrible he had treated her. And how he wouldn't let her have children. He had made her feel so worthless, and the day she finally plucked up the courage to leave him was the best day of her life. Although today was a close second.

Barney told her all about his money problems, and how there were some not very nice people after him for payments. He told her the whole story, including how someone had thrown a brick through his window. He didn't like to tell anyone about his debts, but for some reason felt compelled to tell Alison. His problems were small in comparison to the things she'd been through.

'Well, I hope we're not going to have someone attack us on the way home,' she said, half jokingly, half concerned.

They drank until the pub closed and went back to her house.

Barney said, 'I'd better not drive. I've had too much to drink. I'll phone for a taxi.'

Alison replied, 'Why don't you stay here for the night? I've got a spare room.'

'Yes. That would be great. If you don't mind?'

'Not at all. But I have to go straight to bed. I'm shattered. Thank you so much for coming with me today.' She became overwhelmed with emotion again, so she turned away quickly to hide her fresh tears and hurried to her bedroom.

Out of Order

She went to bed and slept soundly for the first time in six weeks.

26

This morning Barney was suffering the consequences of having a few drinks. It probably hadn't been a great idea, when he thought about what was to come later that evening. But it had been enjoyable all the same and he was pleased it had happened. It was the first time he had met Alison outside of work, or hospitals, other than that brief encounter on the promenade in Brighton, and the conversations were different to the ones they usually had. The alcohol had a lot to do with that.

Alison didn't care that she was suffering a hangover. For the past six weeks she had been waking up with a much worse feeling, and today that weight had been lifted. She was looking forward to work.

They left the house together and drove off to different destinations.

Barney had been given a first job which he could have done without. It sounded like another faulty refrigeration unit, which invariable meant a time-consuming task, working on his knees, and getting dirty. When recovering from a drinking session, all he wanted was five-minute, easy fixes.

He hadn't been for a bacon sandwich this morning and had to settle for a cup of tea from a machine and a packet of crisps. But when he opened the machine door it was like opening an oven door. They had left the machine plugged in even though it had a faulty chiller unit, and that can generate a lot of heat. There were a few hundred bars of chocolate inside which would have to be thrown away. One of the most heartbreaking aspects of the job. But not the crisps. The hot crisps were surprisingly good and he had a second packet, wondering why nobody had thought of it before. He contemplated claiming them as his invention and making a fortune. He could open a shop. 'Barneys Hot Crisps'. That would solve his money worries.

He was feeling uncharacteristically mellow, maybe as a result of the events of yesterday. He decided it was time that he was a bit more tolerant to people that wound him up. Did he really need to be so confrontational with customers? Did it give him satisfaction? The answer to both those questions was probably yes. But nevertheless, he was going to try to deal with people in a different way. He also had to bear in mind that it would only take one phone call from one of these malicious bastards and Richard Bowles would have the excuse he needed to get rid of him. Then he would have even more trouble settling his debts. He had said it all before, but this time he was determined that his new approach of tolerance would be more of a success than it usually was.

The refrigeration job didn't start well. The unit was held in place by a bolt that he couldn't loosen. It was located in a place that made it difficult to get a spanner on it. If there was one thing that got him more frustrated than ignorant customers, it was vending machine designers who had no idea how much misery their ridiculous ideas would cause. Or perhaps they did know, and did it deliberately. Barney often wondered if companies who manufactured vending machines employed someone as a

'Director of Making Things as Difficult as Possible for People Who Have to Use These Things.'

He eventually got the bolt loose, but it involved a fair amount of muttering and cursing. He was still on his knees, covered in grime, and had tools and machine parts strewn around the floor when a young lady walked into the room and asked him an unexpected question.

'Excuse me. Are you here for the job interview?'

To which Barney instinctively replied, 'Yes, of course I am. I just thought I'd ease my nerves by taking your vending machine to pieces while I was waiting.'

The girl didn't look too impressed.'

'Are you being sarcastic?'

Barney quickly got to his feet.

'No, no! I didn't mean it like that. Sorry. Let me start again. No, I'm not here for the job interview. I'm here to repair your vending machine.'

'That still sounds like you're being sarcastic.'

'I know. It's a habit I'm trying to break. Sorry again.'

She walked away. He hoped he had said enough to earn forgiveness.

The being tolerant plan had not got off to a flying start. He left the site feeling guilty. But perhaps that was a good sign. He was feeling empathy with the girl who was no doubt rushing around

Out of Order

in a panic trying to find the correct person who was there for the job interview, and had her boss giving her a hard time. Barney didn't want to make things harder for her, and hoped he hadn't. Maybe there was some hope that he could change after all.

After a few more trouble-free jobs, and several cups of heavily sugared tea, his hangover was clearing away nicely and he was looking forward to the darts match. Just one more job to get through. He turned his phone off to make sure he wasn't sent any more work this time.

His final task of the day threw up another test of his patience. A really big test.

He was sent to a hotel that had a coffee machine in their restaurant, which Barney himself had installed just over a year ago. He introduced himself to the lady sitting at the reception.

'Hello. I'm from Vendetta. I'm here to repair your coffee machine.'

'Your machine is useless. It breaks down every week.'

'It's not my machine. It's your machine.'

'Well... it breaks down every week. What are you going to do about it?'

'That depends. What have you been doing about it when it breaks down? Have you been fixing it yourself?'

'No. We call your company and they send someone to fix it.'

'Really? That's very odd. I normally cover this area and I've not been to this machine since I installed it in October last year. If you could tell me the name of the person who has been coming here every week, I will call him and find out what the problems are you've been having.'

'I don't know his name.'

'He must have signed in?'

'No. He didn't.'

'But you made me sign in. You said nobody was allowed to start work until they've filled in the risk assessment and method statement forms.'

'Erm…'

'Well don't worry. I'll just bring up the machine's history and find out from there.'

A machine's history was a great device. It had allowed him to make a fool of people who were displaying phoney outrage. He pressed a few buttons on his screen and brought up the machine's log of service calls.

'According to this, the last visit from us was 15th August. And the time before that was 23rd January. Two faults have been reported since it was installed. Not exactly "every week" wouldn't you say?'

'I didn't SAY every week.'

'That's exactly what you said.'

'I didn't mean EVERY week.'

'What did you mean then?'

By now she'd run out of replies.

'Shall I just get the machine working?'

Out of Order

He did get the machine working, which wasn't difficult as it didn't have much wrong with it. He took a coffee from it and sat down to drink it, while pondering on the conversation he'd just had. He was going to abandon the tolerance idea. If he had to come face to face with customers like this it could never work. He realised that verbal exchanges of this particular nature were one of the few pleasures of the job. Tying someone who deserves it in knots, and proving to them they were talking bullshit. From now on he was going to be even more acerbic. To hell with Richard Bowles.

He finished his coffee and set off for home to ditch the car and change out of his uniform, then head to the railway station. He was ready for action. But tonight, he was going to get some action he could have done without.

27

He was pleased to have got home early. It gave him plenty of time to change out of his uniform and have a shower. He was still grimy from that first job. But just as he was about to go out of the door, his phone rang. Liam's name flashed up.

'Alright Liam? You're not still at work, are you?'

'You'll never guess where I am?'

'Buckingham Palace?'

'No.'

'Stringfellows?'

'No'

'In that case I'm out of ideas. Enlighten me.'

'I'm at the McLaren formula one headquarters in Woking.'

'I can hardly contain my excitement.'

'You don't sound impressed.'

'I'm not. I think formula one is boring.'

'You're just saying that to get revenge on me for saying Captain Scarlet sounded naff.'

Liam was a big fan of formula one. Barney took the opportunity to wind him up.

'Look at it this way. Imagine if at the Olympic games 100 metres final they gave the fastest runner a ten metre head start and a pair of the best quality running shoes, then gave the second fastest runner a pair of ordinary trainers and he was only given a five metre start, then made the slowest runners start at the back and run in wellies. And the only way the fastest runner could fail to win is if he trips over. Do you think that would be an exciting race? That's what formula one is like.'

Liam took the bait, as usual.

'You're just too stupid to understand it.'

'That' s not true. I do understand it. In fact, there's nothing I like better than falling asleep in front of a Grand Prix on a Sunday afternoon. It usually takes about two laps.'

'You like cricket. There can't be anything more boring than cricket.'

'Yes, there is. That American motor racing you watch. The one with the big oval tracks.'

Yes, I do like it, and it's not boring. It's just too complicated for you.'

'Oh yes, it's really hard to understand. And it must take a lot of skill. Turn the steering wheel slightly to the left and put your foot on the accelerator.'

'Piss off. You've got more rabbit than Sainsburys.'

Barney laughed.

'Oh no! I can't believe you used that phrase. You've been watching too many episodes of Only Fools and Horses. Assuming you know what that is. Have you ever tried buying rabbit in Sainsburys?'

Liam was getting more and more wound up.

'No, I fucking haven't.'

'Well I have. I was dating this very nice Spanish girl, Manuela, and one night I decided to cook her a paella. The recipe said I needed rabbit. I went to Sainsburys. But they didn't have any. I've checked in several other Sainsburys since then. None of them had any rabbit. Therefore, having more rabbit than Sainsburys simply means having any rabbit at all. Even a tiny amount.'

If Liam had been with Barney at this point, he would have punched him in the mouth. Barney sensed this, realised he was going too far, and changed the subject to cool things down. He knew Liam couldn't afford to stay angry for long. Not if he wanted Barney's help.

'I did a job in Pinewood studios last week. Now that's what I call impressive.'

'Did you see any famous actors?'

'Nah. How about you? Did you come across any famous drivers?'

'No. I think they all live in Monte Carlo, or somewhere like that, to avoid paying tax.'

'Have you managed to fix their vending machine?'

'Unfortunately, not. They've got one of those new Cafeblam 73s. I can't get it working. You did the training. That's why I called you. I need your help.'

Barney didn't think he would be able to help. He hadn't taken in much information at the training.

'You'll have to make it quick. I'm on my way out to catch a train.'

'There's a message on the screen saying Change Water Filter, and I don't know how to get rid of it.'

'This is just a wild guess, but maybe it needs the water filter changing?'

'Don't be such a smartarse. And don't talk to me the way you do to your customers. I've already changed the filter. But the message is still on the screen.'

'Then you need to tell the machine you've changed the filter. Press and hold the two buttons on the left. When the screen shows you've entered the program, use the top right button to scroll down until it asks you if you've changed the water filter. Press the bottom right button. Then turn the power off and back on. Then fuck off home!'

'Cheers,' said a grateful Liam.

Barney was impressed with himself. He must have learnt something in Torquay after all.

Then much to his dismay the phone went off again. This time it said 'Mum'.

'Hi mum'

'Hello Cecil. I just rung to see how you are.'

'I'm fine. I'm just dashing out to catch a train. I've got a big darts match tonight.'

'I bought a new table for the dining room today.'

'That's great. Can I talk to you about it tomorrow?'

'You never have time for me. When are you next coming to visit?'

'I was only there two weeks ago. But I'll try and get there around Christmas. I promise. But I really have to dash.'

After the call he felt guilty again, but it was just bad timing on her part. He would call her back tomorrow and she'd be happy. He hoped that would be the last of the interruptions for now. But it wasn't. The phone burst into song yet again. It was Colin. There was no way he was going to talk to Colin today, so he just let it play its tune. When it stopped, it started again immediately.

'Bugger off Colin,' he shouted at the phone without answering it. But the screen didn't say Colin. This time it announced an unknown caller. By now Barney was fuming. He answered it.

'Yes? What is it?'

'We want the rest of the money. All of it.'

He yelled down the phone, 'Get stuffed!'

He ended the call, ran out of the door and ran towards the station, thinking that may not have been a wise thing he had just done.

He ran to the station, but missed the train he was hoping to catch, so much to his annoyance he had to stand on the platform for 25 minutes waiting for the next one.

Out of Order

After an average journey into Paddington and tube to the city, he arrived at the Black Cat and again Daffy and Tom, plus three of the opposition were already there. Tom was heading to the bar and Barney accepted his offer of a pint. Being in the round tonight might not have been the best idea, but it was the last match of the year, so why not?

The remaining players on both sides drifted in and the drinking continued.

The game got underway, and Roy chose himself to play the first singles. It was also the lottery leg. Roy wanted to get it out of the way before everybody was too drunk. Today's numbers would have to be used for the next few weeks when they didn't have any matches.

Barney was playing the fifth game in the singles. He was very drunk by then, which often helped him. Not this time though. He lost. But he redeemed himself while partnering Fiona in the pairs, hitting a nice treble 18, double 16 two dart checkout. Fiona, fuelled by a few glasses of Pinot Grigio, gave him a sloppy kiss on his cheek as a reward. At last, he'd managed to get a kiss from a girl following the failures of recent weeks.

Norfolk and Good eventually won the match 7-4, which meant Mickey Mouse Club were knocked out of the cup. But nobody on either side seemed bothered. By then the whole team were seriously pissed. At 10.30 Daffy had to leave to catch his train. He shook hands with everyone and staggered out of the door, relying on autopilot to get him home. The rest of the team had another pint and then it was Tom's turn to say goodbye. He put on his jacket, and found that it was unusually baggy. Also, there was a gap between the bottom of the jacket and his trousers, and the sleeves ended just below his elbow. Tom was tall and slender. This jacket was the same colour as his, but designed for someone much shorter and stockier. Someone like Daffy for instance. Then the penny dropped. Daffy had gone home in Tom's jacket. They all found it hilarious, until Tom remembered his train ticket, credit card, money, phone, and house keys were in his jacket pocket. Roy tried calling Tom's number, but there was no answer.

Tom was now seriously concerned, but needn't have been. If they all hadn't been so drunk, any of them could have applied a bit of logic and realised that Daffy wouldn't be able to get into the station because his train ticket was back in the pub in his own jacket.

Ten minutes later Daffy lurched back into the pub with a huge grin on his face. He was wearing a jacket that looked like it was squeezing the life out of him. It almost went down to his knees, and his hands were nowhere to be seen due to the extra-long sleeves. The team erupted into laughter. The biggest mystery of this event was, even allowing for the enormous amounts of alcohol consumed, how did Daffy not realise something was wrong when he put the jacket on? And how did none of the others notice it when he was saying his goodbyes? The jackets were returned to the correct owners and everyone headed out of the pub. Most of them made it home unharmed. Most of them.

On the train home, Barney fought hard to stay awake. He had

Out of Order

fallen asleep on previous occasions and had woken up at a variety of stations out in the English countryside. Sometimes there was still time to get a train back down the line depending how long he'd slept, and how late it was. Sometimes he had to get an expensive taxi home. And one time he just fell asleep again on a station platform somewhere near Oxford and woke up in the morning. Fortunately, he managed to stay awake this time, helped by the amusement of the jacket mix up, which caused him to laugh out loud at random intervals, and which in turn amused the other passengers on the train. He got out of the train at Maidenhead Station. His favourite set of darts didn't come with him though. He had inadvertently left them lying on the seat to continue their journey.

All that was left to do was negotiate the walk from the station to his house. Shouldn't be a problem. He'd done it many times before. He could do it in his sleep. Which is virtually what he was doing.

He made it to his front door, fumbled for his key, and was looking forward to bed. He wasn't going to be able to do that just yet. He felt a ferocious blow to the side of his face and fell to the ground. He looked up and saw two figures in the dark. They started kicking him the ribs and stomach. Then they ran off and left him lying there.

28

He had been expecting a hangover, but nothing of this magnitude. There was more pain than usual, and pain in places which weren't in the normal places for a hangover. Then he remembered the assault. He thought about how he was going to respond. The sensible thing to do would be to go to the police. They can't get away with what they did. Or perhaps they could. It could have been a warning. Next time they would do a lot more damage. Telling the police could make it worse. He didn't know. He'd never had dealings with people like this before.

His head and face were hurting like hell, partly from whatever they had hit him with and partly from the booze. His ribs ached a bit, but nowhere near as bad as it could have been. In fact, it felt as if they had only done a half-hearted job on him. He would have thought professional thugs would have caused him more serious damage. Not that he wanted them to. He felt bad enough. It was just strange. He even felt that if he hadn't been so drunk, and wasn't taken by surprise, he would have at least stood a chance of fighting back. Next time he would have to be ready for them.

He felt just about well enough to go to work, but wouldn't be dashing around for anyone. He didn't actually have any work yet because he'd cleared up all his calls the previous afternoon, which meant he could stay at home for a while. Hopefully he could have a quiet couple of hours reading the paper and drinking coffee. A phone call from Mary shattered the illusion.

'Barney. How far are you from Amersham? We need you to go somewhere urgently. Some stupid bastards have phoned up to say they had to call the fire brigade and are blaming our machine. Could you just go there and find out what the fuck they're talking about?'

'Yeah. OK.'

'I've sent Liam there too because it's so urgent and Bowles is getting worked up about it. I don't know which one of you is nearest.'

This was where Barney's years of experience would come in handy. If he took his time getting there Liam would get there first and have to sort the problem out, whatever it was. He put the kettle on.

An hour and a half later he arrived at the site in Amersham. He saw Liam sitting in his car playing some game on his phone. He must be craftier than Barney had given him credit for. He tapped on his window. Liam opened the door and jumped out of his car.

'Bloody hell! What happened to you?'

'I was beaten up last night.'

'I think some of you take these darts games too seriously.'

'No, it didn't happen at the darts, you pillock. They got me at my front door when I was on my way home.'

'Why? What happened? Do you know who it was? Have you called the police?'

Barney was feeling weak and didn't want to talk about it any further.

'OK. Maybe later. Let's go and find out what's been happening in here.'

They both went into the building and a senior manager was called to meet them.

Liam stayed quiet. As usual he was going to let Barney do all the talking, which he thought was unfair given the condition he was in. The manager spoke.

'There was smoke pouring out of the vending machine. We had to call the fire brigade.'

Barney looked up at the smoke alarms. 'Did it set the smoke alarms off?'

'No. I don't think so.'

'Oh. Well either they are not very good smoke alarms, or there can't have been that much smoke.'

The manager wasn't at all impressed by the suggestion.

'There were tons of smoke. We had no choice but to evacuate the room.'

'What did the fire brigade do when they got here?'

'They unplugged the machine and told us to call Vendetta.'

Barney was flabbergasted. 'Are you telling me there was smoke billowing out of the machine and nobody thought to unplug it?'

The manager didn't have an answer.

Barney continued. 'And didn't anyone read the sign on the

machine which gave the instructions to call the number on there if there were any problems with the machine?'

'Well, we thought the fire brigade was a better option because of all the smoke.'

'The smoke would have stopped if someone had unplugged the machine.'

Barney looked inside the machine and found a burnt solenoid on a valve. He asked Liam to go to his car and get a new valve. Liam brought the valve and fitted it while Barney was telling the manager his problem was solved. Then they wandered back to the car park.

Liam asked, 'Do you fancy a pint?'

Barney replied, 'No, sorry. Not today. I'm feeling like shit. I don't think I could even drink one. I'm suffering from having too much last night, along with the thumping I took.

So, they just talked in the car park for a while. Barney told him the details of the assault on him and the reasons behind it. Now there were two people who knew about his financial woes. If it became common knowledge on the Vendetta grapevine, he wouldn't know which of them to blame. Liam offered to find them and give them a good hiding. If only it were as simple as that.

Liam said,' Listen mate, to be honest you're not looking too good. Why don't you go home? I'm sure they can manage without you for one afternoon.'

'Yes. You could be right. I'll give Sweary a call and see how much work we've got on. I'll not tell her what happened. I'll just say I'm feeling ill or something. I have to call her anyway.'

'Do you think your face will be back to normal in time for the Christmas party? It's only eight days away.'

'Yes. I'm sure it will be.'

'Oh no. That must be hugely disappointing for you.'

'Go fuck yourself.'

Liam responded with a small chuckle. He didn't often win the verbal jousts against Barney. But he didn't say anything else. He was genuinely concerned for his friend.

Barney called Mary and told her the story of the fire brigade.

'Fucking morons! Why didn't they just unplug the fucking machine?'

'Why indeed? Anyway Mary. Have we got much work on? I've got a migraine and could do with going home early for a lie down?'

'It isn't too busy at the moment. Just go. We'll manage.'

'OK. Thanks.'

He drove home and found a note pushed through his letterbox. It read, 'You must be more careful how you speak to me. That really wasn't very nice of you. Last night was just for starters. We want payment in full. Or you'll be getting another visit.'

Although it wasn't pleasant to receive it, Barney still felt it was all a bit amateurish. He could take the note to the police. Are they so confident he wouldn't? But again, he wasn't sure if he should. It could be that they deliberately took it easy on him next time they would do a lot more damage. They had changed their demands. Instead of taking relatively small payments which were mostly interest, they were now asking for repayment in full. Somehow he had to pay off the six thousand pounds and get rid of them for good.'

As promised, he phoned his Mum.

'Hi Cecil. Have you got time for me today?'

'Yes. Sorry about yesterday mum. I really did have to dash off.'

'I'll let you off this time. So, how are you?'

'I've got a few problems. Mainly money.'

'I got a bit to spare. Will a hundred pounds help?'

'No. It's very kind of you, but I'll sort it out somehow. How's the new dining room table?'

They chatted for a while about the new table and one or two other things. He promised to visit sometime over the Christmas holidays.

After the call was ended, he felt guilty yet again. His mum was offering him a hundred quid she probably couldn't afford, and it wouldn't even put a scratch in the debt. He had to somehow find a way to sort this out himself. But right now, he couldn't think of anything.

He took some painkillers and went to bed.

29

Barney had spent the weekend recovering from Thursday. He took the opportunity to cut himself off from the world. He'd abstained from any drinking, apart from coffee and tea, and spent the majority of the weekend sleeping, eating, and lazing around in front of the television watching sport and getting through the backlog of trashy programs he had recorded. He hadn't received any telephone calls either, which he was grateful for. The bruising on his face looked pretty bad, and his ribs were still sore, but he was feeling a lot better than he was on Friday. So he set off for work on Monday morning feeling reasonably refreshed.

Shortly after leaving home he pulled up at a red traffic light, and while he was waiting, he saw a man pushing a car. He was trying to push it into a space next to the kerb. He wasn't the biggest of men, and was clearly struggling. A string or cars drove around him, and several pedestrians walked past, mostly with their heads down, and some blatantly staring. This made Barney's blood boil. What the hell is wrong with people? Could not even one of them offer to help him. Barney decided he would. By the time the lights had turned green and he had found somewhere to park, it appeared the man had just about completed his task. He got out of the car anyway and started walking towards the man. But just as the man, puffing and panting, and bent forward with his hands on his knees, had finally managed to get the car into place, the car doors opened and two other men got out. Barney turned around and got back in his car. His faith in humanity had taken another hit.

Out of Order

The next thing he did was pop into the local shop for a newspaper and a few bits and pieces.

He collected the things in a basket and took them to the girl at the till, who scanned the goods and told him 'That'll be £6.34 please.'

His credit card was still out of use. That was a separate debt which would have to be paid off at some stage, but at least Barclaycard were unlikely to send thugs around to beat him up. It was most inconvenient, but he saw little prospect of it being in use in the near future. At least it stopped him buying stuff on the internet that he didn't need. But it just didn't seem right that loan sharks who used violence would have to get paid before a legitimate credit card company, not that they were angels either by any means. Yet another thing wrong with our world, he thought.

He handed the girl a ten-pound note.

'Haven't you got anything smaller?' she snapped.

'Yes, I've got a fiver,'

'Are you trying to be funny?'

'Not at all, five pounds is the next lowest denomination of British currency. Unless they've brought out a seven-pound note without telling anyone?'

This didn't improve her mood very much. But she somehow managed to find the £3.66 and reluctantly handed it over. That's the trouble with the credit card generation. They don't understand how to use cash, even if they work in a shop. But Barney was feeling OK about it. He assumed he could look forward to a trouble-free day now that he'd got his daily encounter with someone obnoxious out of the way early.

Oh no. Not even close!

He headed off to work and did two routine jobs, then remembered where Alison would be at this time on a Monday morning. Just a mile and a half from where he was. He felt a need to go and talk to her. He got there within a few minutes, and could see her van in the loading bay. She wasn't in the building. She was busy unloading boxes of snacks onto a trolley, when she spotted him heading towards her.

She looked at him in horror. 'What the hell's happened to you?'

'I'd rather not talk about it.'

He meant that too. He didn't want her to know he'd been attacked. He'd already told her that he owed money and about the brick thrown through his car window. But he wanted to keep quiet about the assault. He would have to make something up.

'Oh, come on. You were there for me when I needed you. At least let me return the favour.'

He replied, 'Don't give me that old cobblers. You're just being nosey.' Then he immediately regretted saying that.

'Please yourself,' she huffily muttered.

He could tell he had upset her a little with that remark.

'OK. Sorry. I do appreciate your concern. I'll tell you what happened. I was extremely pissed on Thursday night and fell over on the way home. Right on my face. I tried to put my hands out but I was too late.'

'You idiot.'

'Oh, thanks for being there for me. I feel a whole lot better now.'

Now she gave half a laugh, but it wasn't genuine. She was concerned. She wasn't overly convinced by his falling over while drunk tale. She knew there must be something more sinister to it. Something to do with him owing people money perhaps.

'You're not going to look great at the Christmas party. That's not going to disappear in five days.'

'Well, there's not much I can do about it.'

'No, but maybe there's something I can do. I can do wonders with a bit of makeup. I'll meet you on Saturday and sort you out. Then we can travel together if you like?'

'I don't know about makeup. I don't want to look like a girl.'

'You won't look like a girl. I'm not a miracle worker.'

'Do you think it will work?'

'I'm not sure. I've never had to hide something as bad as that. My ex-husband might have been a complete bastard, but his thing was mental torture. He didn't go in for physical abuse. Besides, he was a puny weakling really and I don't know why it took me so long to realise it. If he'd ever laid a finger on me, I would have flattened him.'

Barney believed her. The tenderness and fragility she had displayed over the past six weeks had well and truly gone. She was back to her old self. But that was a good thing, he supposed. The heart attack and eyesight scares had sent her back to being the woman she had been when she was married. Vulnerable and scared. Now she was back to being the strong and independent person she made herself become.

It was time for them to go in separate directions. She said she would call him before the weekend to arrange his makeover session. And he drove off to his next assignment.

That assignment was in a large supermarket in Uxbridge. It was a place he didn't normally cover, but their regular engineer was on holiday. It was another DIY site. He was about to encounter a man who was going to take stubbornness to a whole new level.

'Hello I'm from Vendetta. I'm here to repair your vending machine.'

'I know. I recognise the uniform.'

He took him to the vending machine. It didn't look familiar.

'Right, I'll get on with it then. I don't normally work on this particular model. I'll need to borrow your key.'

'Don't you have your own key?'

'Clearly not. Otherwise, I wouldn't have asked to borrow yours.'

'Our regular engineer has his own key.'

'He's got a couple of days off. If you can wait until Thursday he can come in and do the job?'

'No, we can't wait until Thursday.'

'Well, that's a bit of a problem. If only I could think of a simple solution.'

Barney wasn't going to allow this prat to rile him. He would either have to get the key, or the machine stayed out of order. It wouldn't make any difference to him. Realising he had no choice, the man trudged off to get his keys, grumbling all the way. He deliberately took ages to return. Then he handed Barney a bunch of keys, who looked at them and said, 'The key to the machine isn't on here.'

'Yes, it is.'

'I assure you it isn't.'

'Those are the vending machine keys.'

'I've got an idea. How about this? Why don't you use them to unlock the machine? Then you can make me look really stupid in front of all these people.'

He then tried each key on the bunch without success.

'I know what's happened. I've picked up the wrong keys.'

'You don't say? In front of all these people too. I hope you don't feel too embarrassed.'

Eventually the man had reluctantly opened the machine. After Barney had successfully completed the job and drove away, he couldn't help wondering if everybody had to deal with people like this, or was it just him? He also wondered how the likes of Richard Bowles would react if they had to go out and come face to face with these people. Would he be able to stick with his policy of the customer always being right? Yes, was the most likely answer. As far as Barney was concerned, the man had no principles. He wondered how he slept at night.

30

The answer to that question was he didn't. At least not tonight. Richard Bowles was having trouble sleeping. Which meant his wife wasn't getting much sleep either.

'What's the matter dear? You seem a bit restless tonight.'

'Sorry. It's work. I'm getting really fed up with it. I'm thinking about looking for a new job.'

'What on earth for? I thought you were happy there.'

'I was. But things are getting me down lately. I have to listen to customers complaining all day long. And my own staff have no respect for me.'

'I'm sure that's not true.'

'It is true. I started at the bottom and worked my way up, through lots of hard work. But they don't realise that. They think I don't know what it's like to be out there facing customers. They just think I sit on my backside all day bossing them around.'

There was some truth in what he was saying. But he had hardly worked his way up from the bottom. He wasn't always the boss though. He joined the company as a sales rep, so he did know what it was like coming face to face with customers.

'The ones I had to deal with posed a tougher challenge than the ones the likes of Barnard and Liam face. Everybody believes everything an engineer tells them, but they all think the sales rep is lying all the time. It's just not fair.'

Out of Order

His wife had never heard him talking like this before. Come to think of it, she had noticed he had been unusually moody lately. She went downstairs and brought back a pot of tea. She thought it might do him good to get it all off his chest.

He poured himself a cup of tea and continued. 'I get complaints all day long from people who are in a rage because their coffee machine doesn't work. I always try to be polite to them, and do my best to solve their problems, even though it's not always easy. But some of my staff aren't quite so polite to them.'

His wife would much rather go back to sleep, but she was going to be the dutiful wife, listening to her husband, and chipping in with what she thought were encouraging comments.

'How do you know?' she asked.

'Because they phone me to complain about them. There's one particular engineer who I receive complaints about almost every week. They say he's rude to them, and makes them look stupid. He's a nightmare. I want to sack him, but you can't do that so easily these days.'

'Why do you think he does it?'

'Well, he would say the customers are rude and condescending to him, and he refuses to accept being treated that way. He is so unreasonable.'

'He doesn't sound unreasonable. I would say he's got a point. Your staff have a right to carry out their work without being subject to that sort of treatment. And as their manager you have a duty to give them some sort of protection.'

'So, you're taking their side?'

'Aren't you all supposed to be on the same side?'

'Yes. But try telling them that.'

'If I had to take sides, I'll always be on your side dear. But I'd like to go back to sleep now. Try not to worry about it. How about taking a holiday? Do you think that would help?'

'What, like a weekend in Cornwall or something?'

'In December? No, I was thinking more along the lines of two weeks in the Canary Islands.'

'I can't risk being away from work for two weeks. It would be chaos without me. And we're not made of money. And that's another thing. They think I'm paying myself a fortune while they earn peanuts.'

'Don't you think they might have a point?'

She soon fell back to sleep. But he couldn't. He lay awake tossing and turning for most of the night. He now regretted bringing up the subject with his wife. Her words were hardly supportive. He knew what would solve his problems. He needed to get rid of that pain in the arse Barnard. He was already on his final warning. He was bound to go too far sooner or later.

He would have slept a lot better if only he'd know how close his wishes were to coming true. Barney was very soon to have a confrontation which could potentially bring to an end his employment at Vendetta.

Twenty miles away, Mary was having no such trouble sleeping. She was probably having a dream about the Christmas party on Saturday. She considered herself a real party animal and was looking forward to it immensely.

Out of Order

She had been at Vendetta for just under two years, so she joined a week too late for the party two years ago, and had to miss last year due to suffering from flu. She was especially looking forward to meeting people who she had only spoken to on the phone many times, but had never actually met. The staff who are always out on the road occasionally popped into the depot to pick up supplies or equipment or to have meetings with the management, so she'd seen some of them. A motley bunch mostly, and boring too, but there were a few good-looking ones who passed by now and again. She'd long given up on Barney. They'd had a fun time at the races, but it became obvious to her that they weren't suited to be a couple. They were both abrasive characters and if they were a couple, would no doubt spend all their time together fighting. But it meant they got along great as friends.

Mary was single at present. She hadn't had much success with relationships. She'd had plenty of dates and one-night stands, but nothing ever lasted. Her extrovert personality intimidated men, and her looks hampered her slightly. She wouldn't have accepted that though if someone had dared mention it. She thought she was gorgeous. It wasn't her intention to meet anyone at the party, but if it happened, it happened. And if it didn't, it was their loss, not hers.

A further ten miles away, Colin was asleep. If Colin was awake, he'd be looking forward to the Christmas party too. Probably. There's nothing much else to say about Colin. If he was a character in Red Dwarf, he would be the one who for no reason keeps phoning up the unpopular guy who repairs the vending machine.

Elsewhere, Alison and Liam both slept soundly. Barney was having trouble sleeping. He wasn't feeling good at all. He couldn't help staring at the doors and windows in case someone came in. His money situation was getting desperate. And he was also concerned about work. He couldn't see the funny side any more. He was close to breaking point.

31

Liam hadn't been doing the job for very long. He was previously working in a shop and had been becoming increasingly fed up with it. He wanted to do a job where he wasn't stuck in the same building all day. A job which provided a company car. He had applied to be an engineer because he thought he was useful when it came to DIY. He assumed vending machines couldn't be all that sophisticated. It came as quite a shock when he discovered how unnecessarily complicated vending machines could be. And how many different varieties there were. He didn't have the qualifications and experience of his friend Barney, but was confident of making a success of it. He was in that early phase in his career where he was eager to keep everybody happy.

When it came to 'customer relations' he'd had no real problems so far. Barney must be just unlucky. Or more likely unnecessarily confrontational. It helped that he was more intimidating than Barney due to his size. Irate customers weren't so keen to pick an argument with him. But it was just a matter of time before he found out what a pain some of them could be. That time had arrived.

He was sent to a job in a bus depot. There was a rest area for the drivers in a little hut, and they had a large hot drinks machine taking up a lot of the very limited space. There were a few drivers squeezed in there too. Even though the fault was simple enough to solve, just removing the faulty sugar canister and putting a new one in, this was not going to be an easy job. For a start he couldn't open the door properly because there was a table and chairs in the way, and there were bus drivers sitting on the chairs. Then when he was doing a contortionist act trying to remove the old canister, someone barged into him and didn't say a word. Liam had a few words to say about it though, but all he got back was a scowl.

He took the canister out and went back to his car to find a new one. He was parked about 200 metres away, but took his time because he wanted to calm down. He was gone for less than ten minutes altogether. He was relieved to find the bus drivers had gone, so he fitted the new sugar canister in peace, tested the machine, went back to his car and drove away.

Half an hour later he was about to start his next job when his phone played a tune. The screen said 'Richard'. He hadn't had enough problems with Bowles yet to have bothered to program in an offensive nickname like Barney had done. He answered and Richard spoke.

'Liam. We've had a complaint about you. They are saying you went outside and left the machine door open, putting their staff in danger.'

Liam was taken aback. He'd never heard anything like this before. In fact, he was so shocked that uncharacteristically he went on the offensive.

'That's rubbish. I left the door open while I went to the car for a spare part. They weren't in any danger. I'd unplugged the machine at the wall. And even if I hadn't, the only way they could put themselves in any danger would be if they stuck their hands inside the machine and started poking around with the wires. Which would be their own fault.'

Bowles was still not backing the staff, despite the midnight advice from his wife.

'I'm afraid it doesn't work that way Liam. You are responsible for people's safety while you're working.'

'They were safe. I'd unplugged the power. The only reason they've complained is because I had a go at one of them for barging into me while I was working. Which incidentally is a far more dangerous thing to do than what I'm being accused of.'

'Well try to be more careful in future. After all, these are the people who pay our wages.'

Liam was fuming. But also proud for sticking up for himself. Barney would be proud of him too. He'd been warned about this kind of thing by Barney, but thought he was exaggerating. Evidently, he wasn't.

Barney was meeting him later today to help him with a job he was having a spot of bother with. He was looking forward to telling him all about this morning's events.

They met up later at a hotel in Marlow.

The hotel was in a picturesque setting next to the Thames. It was like a scene on a postcard. There was a little bridge with boats going by, and swans everywhere. Even the sun was shining. The hotel itself looked very plush. They suspected it would cost more than they could afford to stay there for a night. They went to the reception and because Liam had already been to the machine, and knew where it was, they were allowed to proceed without an escort. They had to pass through a bar which overlooked the water.

'This would be a good place to have a pint when we've finished,' suggested Liam. He was eager to sit down and tell him about the events of this morning.

Barney didn't agree. 'Have a look at the prices.'

Liam looked. Then agreed if they were having a drink it would be somewhere else.

He led them down some stairs into a grotty looking basement. They had a large hot drinks machine which had seen better days. Barney had observed on previous jobs in the Hilton and the Ritz, the posher the hotel, the worse the facilities were for the staff.

Barney asked, 'So what difficulties are you having with this one?'

Liam replied, 'They tell me it's leaking. Sometimes they say there's water all over the floor. And sometimes there isn't. But the inside of the machine is bone dry, and I can't find any leaks. Apparently, it was really flooded last week. But it has been OK since then.'

'Strange.' said Barney.

They sat down and risked a cup of tea from the machine.

Liam told him the story of the bus garage. Barney kept a straight face.

'You really ought to be more tolerant. Haven't you heard that the customer is always right?'

'Bollocks!'

'Exactly. Well, I'm glad to hear you're coming around to my way of thinking.'

Which was partly true. He was glad. But at the same time, he was infuriated on Liam's behalf. He changed the subject.

'Anyway. Are you going to tell me who this mystery woman you're chasing after at the Christmas party?'

'Oh, alright then. But don't tell anyone. It's Mary.'

Barney spluttered a mouthful of tea all over his shirt. 'Really? Are you serious?'

'Yes.'

'Sweary?'

'Yes. What's wrong with that?'

'Nothing. I just didn't think she was your type. Who am I kidding? Everybody is your type.'

'Bollocks again!'

Liam sulked for a few minutes and said nothing. Barney said, 'Do you know I took her to Windsor races at the end of the summer?'

'No. You kept that quiet.'

'There was nothing to tell. It wasn't a date or anything. But she's good fun.'

Liam was quiet for a moment. A question was whirring around in his head.

'So, what does she look like?'

Barney instinctively started to describe her, but then stopped in his tracks when he realised what Liam had just said.

'What? Are you telling me you've never even met her?'

'No, I haven't. But I've talked with her many times. I like her for her personality. She makes me laugh. We aren't all as shallow as you and just care about looks.'

'If you say so.'

Liam paused for a few more moments. Then asked, 'So what does she look like?'

Barney told him, 'She's, sort of... Erm... well, you know. She's got a good personality. She makes you laugh. That's all that matters. She must be about five years older than you.'

'So? '

'You like older women then?'

'I like all women, remember?' said Liam with indignation.

They finished their drinks and Barney said, `Come on. Let's get out of here.'

'But what about the leaky machine?' asked Liam.

'Oh, I solved that while we were drinking our tea.'

'How did you manage that? Where was the water coming from then?'

'The Thames.'

'What do you mean?'

'The Thames. It's a big river. You might have noticed it on the way in. You also may have heard on the news about all the floods last week? Rivers bursting their banks? Your leak was the river Thames coming up through the floorboards.'

'Amazing, how did you manage to figure that out?'

'Elementary my dear Liam.'

'What are you on about now?'

'Let me guess. You've never heard of Sherlock Holmes either? He's a detective. He wears a ridiculous hat, smokes a pipe and always has a magnifying glass in his hand. I bet you think he's naff?'

'I know who Sherlock Holmes is. Stop taking the piss.'

They had a beer in the bar after all despite the prices, because it was such a pleasant setting. Barney offered to pay, but he had an ulterior motive. He had a job scheduled for the next day that he didn't particularly want to do. He intended to take advantage of Liam's naivety.

Barney asked him, 'Have you been anywhere else interesting lately?'

Liam said, 'I did a job in a prison yesterday. Or a young offender's institution, to give it it's official title. You could say it was interesting, but not very nice. How about you?'

'Yes. I've been to the Mars factory in Slough.'

'What's that like?'

'It smells of chocolate. Then they give you a big bag of assorted chocolate bars when you leave.'

'Wow, that's terrific. Just what someone who works with vending machines is desperately in need of. Free chocolate.'

Barney was steadily working the conversation to where it needed to be to suit his ulterior motive.

'I was doing a job in a place in Hayes a few weeks ago. It's called the Vinyl Factory. I think it was something to do with HMV. They started off around there somewhere. I love it when I get sent to a job in there. They've got this huge wall which is covered in thousands of 45rpm singles covers. I usually stay there for ages looking at them and spotting the ones I've got in my record collection.'

Liam wasn't impressed. 'I don't have a record collection. I download all of my music. You see, there's this thing called the internet.'

'Sounds a bit naff to me,' said Barney.

'I'll try to explain it to you if you want, grandad.'

'Downloads can never replace the feeling I used to get when walking out of the Virgin Megastore in Oxford Street with the latest LP by one of my favourite bands in my hand. By the time I was at the end of my teens, you couldn't buy vinyl. It's just not the same without it.'

'Yeah, yeah,' said Liam. 'I used to feel the same about CDs. But you've got to move with the times.'

But Barney wasn't finished with the nostalgia. 'My gran used to have a gramophone.'

'What the hell's a gramophone?'

'It's a sort of old-fashioned CD player. But the discs weren't so compact. I was about 8 years old. I asked her if I could try it. She said I could, but I couldn't find a plug. She told me it didn't work with electricity. You had to wind it up with a handle. I thought she'd gone nuts, but it turned out she was right. I wound the handle, and this turntable started whizzing around at what looked like roughly 78rpm. I put on one of her records and applied this vicious looking metal spike to it. I almost hit the ceiling with the racket that came out. There was no volume control. No wonder most old people are hard of hearing. Speaking as an electrical engineering graduate, I still can't understand how that thing could make so much noise without electricity. But some of those old records must have been worth a fortune. There was an original Rock Around the Clock by Bill Hailey and his Comets. And a few others too. If my gran had left me those in her will instead of chucking them in the bin, I wouldn't be getting beaten up by people I owe money to.'

Liam was getting bored. Barney thought it was time to get to the point.

'I've got a job at Warner Bros studios near Watford tomorrow.'

'Oh, wow! That's where they filmed parts of the Harry Potter movies. I've always wanted to go there.'

'I'm not such a big Harry Potter fan. Besides, I've already been there several times. I'm more than happy to let you go instead of me. I'll tell Mary to transfer the call to you if you like?'

'Oh thanks. Much appreciated.'

'No problem. But that's another favour you owe me.'

Liam was happy. Barney was happy. Not to mention devious.

32

While he felt some sympathy for Liam after he got into bother with a customer through no fault of his own yesterday, Barney felt some relief that it was possible to happen to someone other than him. Richard Bowles had someone else to pick on for a while. Sadly, it was to be a short-lived relief. He was already feeling like he'd had enough and just wanted to give it all up. He was about to encounter someone who would send him over the edge. And it was to be Barney's step too far that Bowles had been waiting for.

The day started gently enough. His first two jobs were drippy valves. Drippy valves were the vending machine engineer's equivalent of an open goal in football. It couldn't really go wrong. Or shouldn't. Just clean out a bit of limescale, test a few drinks, and be in and out in half an hour. Which meant he'd put two scores on the board and was halfway through Friday morning without breaking sweat.

His next call however, was to prove somewhat more complicated.

The job was at another one of those places he hadn't been to before. He was helping out one of his colleagues who was loaded down with work. But he wasn't there long before he knew why the usual engineer was reluctant to go there. There was no reception desk. He had to press a button with a bell symbol on it and speak to an intercom. Then the door was opened by a pompous looking man with a face like a smacked arse. Barney started off politely enough, but the opening line he got back from him was hardly welcoming.

'Good morning. I'm from Vendetta. I've come to fix your vending machine.'

'About time.'

'What's it doing wrong?'

'It's doing exactly the same as it was the last time.'

'I've never been here before. I don't know what it was doing wrong the last time.'

'I've already told your company what's wrong with it. I explained to them on the phone in great detail.'

'Well, I could phone them and ask them what it was you told them, but it would save a lot of time and effort if you could just tell me.'

'I don't see why I should.'

'Because my mind reading skills are not what they used to be?'

Barney by now was getting a bit peeved. He pretended to make a phone call, and pretended to hang up after five minutes.'

I've tried calling our customer help desk service coordinator, but I'm not getting an answer. Would you just like to tell me what's wrong with your machine?'

'I don't see why I should.'

'In that case there's no point in me staying here any longer. Goodbye.'

'I don't like your attitude.'

'It's your own attitude that you need to be thinking about.'

Barney couldn't get out of there quickly enough. He was gobsmacked. He'd had to deal with some stubborn sods, but this was something else. He drove away and tried to forget it, but his instinct told him this one would be rearing its ugly head again.

Sure enough, around about two o'clock, while Barney was doing what he assumed would be his last call of the week and was anticipating an early finish, his phone sprang into action. He instinctively knew without looking what name would be displayed. Grumbling Bowels! His instinct was correct.

'Hello Cecil. I've had a phone call from one of our customers which I am frankly not happy about. He is saying you refused to repair his vending machine.'

'That isn't true. I was ready and willing to fix it, but he refused to tell me what was wrong with it. He's a nutcase.'

'You cannot go around referring to our customers as nutcases. I need you to go back and sort it out. Now!'

'And how exactly am I supposed to do that? I don't know what's wrong with it. Do you know what's wrong with it?'

'No. I don't.'

'Well how about this? Call him back and do some more crawling. See if he's willing to tell you. Then pass this elusive piece of information on to me, and I'll see what I can do?'

Bowles wasn't thrilled with the suggestion, but knew he didn't have much choice. Even he knew Barney was in the right this time. He hung up, then called again ten minutes later.

'OK. I've spoken to him again. He's willing to allow you back on site.'

'How kind of him.'

'Now, will you get back there as soon as possible.'

'That depends. Did you manage to get him to reveal the nature of his complaint?'

'Yes. He says the coffee is not hot enough.'

'Oh my god! Those poor people. I'd better get there immediately. Could you arrange a police escort for me with a siren and flashing lights? Do you think we should ask the government declare a nationwide state of emergency?'

'You are treading on very thin ice Cecil. And we'll be talking about this again on Monday. I don't have time for this now. Just get back there and sort it out.'

Barney did get there in a hurry. It was Friday afternoon and he wanted to get home. Otherwise, he might have taken a very long route to get there, with a few stops on the way. At least he now knew what they were complaining about. Increasing the temperature is quick and easy. Just a few presses of buttons.

Drink temperature has always been a contentious issue in the world of vending machines. He had seen people drinking coffee that was hot enough to burn their tongue off and still say it was cold. He had seen people take a cup of tea from the machine back to their desk and leave it standing there for fifteen minutes, then drink it and say it wasn't hot enough. And he'd lost count of the number of times when someone was complaining their drinks weren't hot enough and he pretended to increase the temperature, but in fact didn't do anything.

'There. Try it now.'

'Ah yes. That's much better. Thanks.'

He didn't know how this was going to play out, but he wasn't going to take any more crap from this idiot. Realistically he was in the wrong frame of mind to do this job. The sensible thing to do would have been to walk away and come back on Monday. But he wasn't in a position to apply common sense. He was a ticking time bomb waiting to go off.

He rang the bell, spoke to someone on the intercom, and again the door was opened by the same pompous looking man who still had a face like a smacked arse.

'So, you've decided to come back to repair our machine?'

'No. I didn't decide. Someone else decided on my behalf. I would have happily stayed away.'

'Did they tell you what the problem is this time?'

'Yes. The information was relayed to me through an unnecessary series of phone calls. I believe there's some problem with the drink temperature.'

'Yes. It isn't hot enough.'

He was so close to asking him how difficult it had been to say those few words, but he acted with restraint, for the moment.

They went to the machine and Barney started by selecting a black coffee. It felt very hot to him, but at this stage he said nothing. He opened the machine door and accessed the program. The temperature was set at 96°C which was the maximum this particular machine could be set at. Then he had a look at the sensor reading. The screen told him the boiler was in fact at 96°C as expected. He vended another coffee and put his thermometer in the cup. It was reading 93°C, which again was roughly what he expected. The liquid temperature drops slightly when it's taken from the boiler and put in a cup, but it was still easily as hot as a cup of coffee needs to be. He showed this to the man, who wasn't having any of it.

'I'm telling you the drinks are not hot enough and I want you to do something about it!'

That was the moment. Barney had finally flipped. He vended another coffee and handed it to him.

'Here's a coffee. Stick your knob in it.'

'I beg your pardon?'

'Why don't you stick your knob in it, if you can find it? If you manage to keep it in there for ten seconds, I'll accept it isn't hot enough. And if you're still not happy, I'll throw a cup of coffee right in your ugly face and then you can tell me how hot you think it is then, you pompous twat.'

'How dare you? I'll be reporting you to your superiors.'

'Of course you will. That's how pathetic losers like you get your thrills. You've got nothing more interesting to do in your sad existence than to try to make other people as fucking miserable as you are. And for your information, I don't have superiors. Nobody is my superior. Especially that bellend who has the nerve to call himself my boss.'

'I think you'd better leave now.'

'With pleasure.'

Barney walked out of the building feeling euphoric. He had enjoyed that immensely. But the feeling didn't last long. There was a strong, cold breeze which snapped him out of his temporary state of triumph.

He stood next to his car in the cold wind and contemplated his situation. It wasn't good. Nothing is going well for him lately.

As he was putting his tool bag back in the car, he spotted a piece of paper blowing across the car park towards him. That was another thing that got him wound up. Litter bugs. He just couldn't begin to understand how people could go for a picnic in the countryside or to the beach, and walk away leaving bottles and cans lying on the ground when they left. He would normally refuse to pick up someone else's litter. So, it was unusual that he did it this time. Perhaps it was just instinct from his cricket playing days. As the piece of paper was whizzing past him, he swooped down and caught it with one hand. Then he looked at it. Joseph Mallord William Turner was staring back at him. He'd just fielded a twenty-pound note.

Twenty pounds was hardly going to make any difference to his economic woes. He could get four pints of lager with it around these parts, or maybe five if he went to the right pub. But it was a significant moment. At a time when he thought everything was going wrong for him, a sign that your luck can change in an instant was just the tonic he needed.

Barney drove away imagining the phone call that was taking place right now. But he wasn't going to face the consequences today. He turned his phone off and went home. The Christmas party tomorrow was going to be even more interesting now. He didn't expect Richard Bowles to be buying him a drink.

33

This promised to be one of the more eventful weekends of Barney's life. There was the Christmas party tonight, which he was looking forward to, but at the same time was a little apprehensive. For a start Richard Bowles would be there and following the phone call he would have received late on Friday afternoon, wouldn't be in much of a mood for partying. But Barney wasn't going to let that spoil things for him.

There was one other small matter that could put a downer on things. The demand for him to pay off his debts. They wanted the full six thousand pounds this weekend, and there was no way he could get his hands on money like that. He had no idea when or where they would appear, and what action they would take. He was determined to have a good time and get legless tonight no matter what, and if he ended the weekend jobless, limbless, or lifeless, so be it.

The morning passed by without incident. He couldn't help having the occasional glance out of the window, but never saw anybody. All was quiet. Then just after noon the doorbell rang. But much to his relief it was only Alison. She got out her makeup bag and set to work on his face. The bruising had turned a dark shade of blue, and he thought this would be a pointless exercise. At first, he felt a bit silly sitting there getting stuff rubbed on his face. But after a while he was beginning to relax and found he was enjoying it. He didn't fully understand why, but presumably having a woman's hands touching him at long last had a lot to do with it. When it was all done, she put up a mirror in front of him. He was impressed. It didn't hide everything, but it certainly was a big improvement.

'Hey, that's not bad. Not perfect, but not bad.'

'An artist can only work with the materials she's got. You know what they say? You can put lipstick on a pig, but it would still be a pig.'

'Charming.'

'My pleasure. Do you want anything else doing while I'm here? A bit of eye shadow maybe?'

'No thanks. We'll leave it at that.'

He brought them tea and biscuits and they sat down and talked. He told her about the events at work yesterday. She didn't say much, but was concerned for him. She couldn't see him surviving this one. What he said to that man would most certainly be classified as gross misconduct. Then they discussed plans for the evening. Although the company were paying for minibuses to get them home, they would have to make their own arrangements to get there.

Barney said, 'I'm planning on getting a train around five o'clock. Liam and I are going to have a few pints in Canary Wharf before we go to the party. There's some good bars down by the waterside'

'That's a bit early for me. I'm going to go back home and take my time getting ready. I told Mary I would meet her somewhere before we go to the venue. So, I'll be getting a train at about seven o'clock.'

'Liam told me he has got his eye on Mary.'

'No. Seriously?'

'Yes. But when I say eye, I really mean he's got his ear on her. He's never actually met her. His attraction is based purely on the things she says on the phone. Which is usually a string of expletives.'

Alison laughed. She asked, 'What do you think she'll say when she finds out?'

'Probably, fucking fuck, for fucks sake, or something along those lines.'

'No, I mean do you think he's got a chance?'

'Who knows? But it should be interesting to watch.'

Just before half past four she said was going home to get ready. He asked her if she wouldn't mind dropping him off at the railway station. He thought there was less chance of him getting attacked while he was with someone else. Especially if he was in a van rather than walking. It would be such a shame to get another battering after all the work she'd done on his face.

He got on a train at ten past five, and was surprised to see how packed the train was. He regularly caught the train into London during the week and the carriages were fairly quiet. He supposed most people having a night out in London in midweek were already there during the day for work. But this was a Saturday, and he would have to stand up all the way to Paddington.

He emerged from the Canary Wharf Docklands Light Railway station at twenty past six and called Liam, who had arrived ten minutes ahead of him. He had found a pub he liked and Barney told him to have a pint of lager ready.

When Barney walked into the pub, the first thing Liam said was, 'What the hell have you done to your face?'

'What do you mean?'

'Two days ago, you were covered in horrendous bruises. Now they've almost gone.'

'I'll tell you if you promise not to laugh.'

'OK. I promise.'

Barney told him about the makeover session. Liam instantly broke his promise.

'So much for promising not to laugh.'

'I know. But I don't care. You stitched me up yesterday.'

'I don't know what you mean,' said Barney, faking innocence.

'Warner Bros studios. It was a horrible job, and you knew fine well it was going to be. You tricked me into going there, you sneaky bastard.'

'Did you get to meet Harry Potter?'

Alison and Mary met in a different pub not too far away. Alison got a glass of red wine and Mary was on the Bacardi and Cokes. They inevitably started off chatting about work.

Alison asked, 'So how's life in the office?'

Mary told her, 'There's one bit of gossip going around. Let's just say, someone heard someone else having a conversation about something today.'

'Wow! That's shocking. That… Err. Do you think you could give me a bit more on that?'

'How well do you know Barney?'

'Quite well. I did his makeup for him today.'

'You did fucking what?'

'I'll tell you about it in a minute. Why did you ask how well I know him?'

'It's just that someone heard someone else say something about him.'

'Oh, bloody hell Mary. This is like trying to get blood out of a stone. Just tell me what you've heard.'

'Richard Bowles Is going to fire Barney. Tonight.'

'How do you know.'

'I don't. It's just gossip.'

'So, it's probably not even true.'

'No. It's true! Definitely.'

Alison resisted the temptation to tell Mary the bit of gossip she'd heard about Liam and his intentions. But she decided to keep it to herself for the moment. Now there was something else that was going to be interesting to watch.

Back in the other pub Barney was telling Liam about the

incident yesterday. Liam showed more sympathy than he would normally do. His own run in with Bowles had something to do with that. But he still told Barney he'd gone over the top this time.

'You must be mad! Even if you hadn't already had a verbal and written warning, that will be seen as gross misconduct. You'll be sacked. Alright, be a bit cheeky to them, but you can't tell them to stir a cup of coffee with their dick.'

'I know. But this bloke was such a knobhead. I was within a whisker of throwing the coffee in his face.'

'That's going to be your defence, is it? At least I didn't throw boiling coffee in his face, Your Honour.'

On that note Barney told Liam to finish his drink and head to the party. Why waste any more of their own money, something of which was in short supply, when there was booze paid for by the company waiting for them.

Alison and Mary arrived at half past eight. Barney and Liam wandered in at ten to nine. The party was in full swing by then. All four of them were keeping an eye on Richard Bowles, but he was too busy to notice. He was surrounded by the usual crowd of sycophants.

As the night went on and everyone was getting more and more drunk at the company's expense, Alison was getting concerned about what Mary had told her. He wouldn't sack him at a Christmas party. Would he? Even he couldn't be that mean.

Out of Order

She was on the dancefloor with a group of her fellow operators, while at the same time watching Barney who was standing across the other side of the room on the edge of the dance floor being talked at by another engineer. Judging by the look on Barney's face which suggested he wanted to shoot himself, she assumed that must be Colin. Eventually Colin wandered off, leaving Barney on his own. That was when it all started happening.

Richard Bowles started walking purposefully over towards Barney. Alison stopped dancing and just watched from a distance. Bowles reached Barney, but she couldn't see if he'd said anything to him. Then Barney appeared to faint and went crashing to the ground, and his beer glass flew out of his hand. Alison ran over to them and yelled at Bowles.

'Did you have to do that now you heartless bastard? Couldn't you at least have waited until Monday?'

Bowles was stunned by her outburst. None of his staff had ever spoken to him like that before. They were often cheeky or argumentative, but never this angry.

'I'm... I'm sorry Alison, I don't know what you mean.'

'Giving someone the sack at a Christmas party. How could you?'

'I haven't given anyone the sack. I never said a word to him. He just toppled over.'

Alison bent down and looked at Barney's face. He looked to be in a trance. Not too sure where he was. Then he managed to mutter something.

'Alison. Will you marry me?'

'Don't be so bloody ridiculous. Did you land on your head when you fell?'

A broad grin came across his face.

Richard and Alison helped him up and sat him in a chair. Then Richard walked away, feeling flustered following Allison's verbal onslaught.

Barney's grin turned into laughter. Alison was now convinced he had concussion.

'I'm going to call an ambulance.'

She fumbled around in her handbag, before realising her phone must be in the pocket of her coat which was hanging up on the other side of the room.

Barney was still laughing.

'You can use my phone,' he suggested. 'I'm not sure where it is though. I must have dropped it when I fell.'

She looked around and saw it lying on the floor. It had travelled quite far. She retrieved it and tried to hand it to him. But he didn't take it. He just sat there still grinning like an idiot.

She pressed a button and was about to call 999. The screen lit up. She saw a text message from someone called Roy. It said, 'We've won the lottery! Twelve million pounds!'

34

The clock was showing half past eleven when Barney woke up. He was feeling rough. His head was throbbing and his stomach was queasy. The sun was shining through a small gap in the curtains, so he deduced it must be Sunday morning. He also recognised that he was in his own bed. He was hazy on anything else. There'd been times before when he'd got so drunk there were a few details he couldn't recall. But at the moment he couldn't remember anything. He was confident it would all come back to him later. But for now, he just needed a bit more sleep. So, he rolled over to get more comfortable and to turn away from the sun. And saw Alison asleep in bed with him. Even though this took him by surprise, he was in no condition to piece it all together yet. He fell back to sleep within a few minutes.

Almost an hour later Alison woke up and was equally taken by surprise. She also had a touch of amnesia, but knew she'd be able to figure it all out in a while. Her first question was whether they had sex or not, but assumed they had. This concerned her greatly. Not that she was necessarily against the idea. It was just that never in her life had she got so drunk that she'd had sex with someone and couldn't remember. But her immediate priority was to go to the toilet first, and then get a drink of water. She threw back the duvet and was instantly given the answer to the first question. Because she still had all her clothes on. Except her shoes. Barney had all his clothes on too. Including his shoes.

She found the toilet, then stumbled towards the kitchen, where she had a big drink of water. On the way there she passed over quite a few empty beer cans and wine bottles, that certainly weren't there when she was here yesterday afternoon. She also couldn't understand why she wouldn't have slept in the spare bedroom. Come to think of it she couldn't understand why she was here at all. It was never her intention. Again, one of those questions was soon answered.

She heard voices and laughter, which she recognised, coming from the spare bedroom. She tapped gently on the door and was invited in. Liam and Mary were lying in bed intertwined. They had clearly had more success than Barney and Alison at getting undressed, as their clothes were strewn all over the floor, and there was little doubt what they'd been up to. Mary filled her in on a few details of the evening and most of it was coming back to her anyway.

She told her, 'We got into the minibus and when we got to Barney's house, he invited us in and we kept drinking all night.'

'I'd worked out that much. How did the sleeping arrangements come about?'

'It just seemed the natural thing to do.'

'No, I didn't mean you two. I meant for me.'

'Oh, what you get up to is your own business, my dear,' said Mary suggestively.

Meanwhile Barney was waking up again. Alison wasn't there after all. It must have been all a dream. He also had a vague dream about winning the lottery, and had memories of Roy sending him a text. It must have been a wind up. Why would he send a text with such big news? Surely, he would have phoned. He needed the toilet too and was taken aback when he walked past the mountain of empty drink containers. What had been happening here?

He dashed back to his bedroom to find his phone and discovered there were four missed calls from Roy which he had received earlier in the evening. He obviously hadn't heard his phone due to the music at the party. There were missed calls from some of the others in the darts team too. And voicemails. He played them all, then called Roy. They had indeed won the lottery. Six of them would be sharing twelve million pounds. Two million each!

An hour and a half later they had all showered and were sitting around the kitchen table having breakfast, taking turns to recount their memories of the night before.

Then Alison asked Barney, 'So what are you going to do now? I mean work wise.'

'I'm going to go straight to the office tomorrow morning and tell Bowles where to stick his job.'

'You'd better hurry then,' Mary warned. 'He's going to fucking fire you anyway.'

Liam chipped in. 'Hey, I've just thought of a great idea. If you really want to get revenge on him, I could tell him where to stick his job too. All you have to do is give me enough money so I don't have to work ever again.'

'Yes, that would work for me too,' said Mary.

'Nice try. Don't worry. I'll be giving a few gifts to friends and relatives. I just need a bit of time to get my head around it.'

They sat for a while in silence finishing their breakfast. Then the Sunday peace was shattered when a brick came through the window, sending shards of glass flying around the room, and someone kicked on the door until it crashed open. Barney rushed to the door and was thrown back inside by two thugs, presumably the same two who attacked him last week. One of them looked to be in his early twenties, and the other one about forty. Barney had a feeling he'd seen him before, but couldn't remember where. He'd got a slight glimpse of him when they attacked him previously, but he'd also seen him somewhere else.

The older one was clearly in charge. The younger of the two threw a punch at Barney, but he managed to deflect most of the blow. Mary screamed. She didn't really feel the need to. It was pure instinct brought on by years of watching television and old films where the women's role is to stand by watching and screaming while the men fight. Which was ironic because Mary was more likely to win a fight than Barney.

The two intruders ignored her and started shoving Barney around. He swung a punch of his own which connected squarely on the young one's jaw, and he fell to the floor. He took the opportunity to exact some revenge for the kicks in the ribs they had given him with some well-aimed kicks of his own.

Then the older one pulled out a gun and pointed it at Barney. Mary screamed again, this time louder and with more conviction. All of a sudden, things had got more menacing. This man looked like he really meant business. They were now seriously in fear for their lives. For what seemed like an eternity, they all stared at each other in silence.

During this standoff, Barney remembered where he'd seen him before. He'd seen him struggling to push a car a few days ago, and had almost helped him. The two men who had sat in the car while he pushed it were clearly higher up in the organisation.

Strange thoughts can go through a person's mind when they think they're going to die. Mary was terrified. Not to mention a bit peeved. She'd finally met someone who she really connected with. Liam could be the one she could have a long-term relationship with. But depending what this man with the gun does next, it could turn out to be yet another one night stand.

Alison wasn't feeling quite so scared. Perhaps it was because so many bad things had happened to her lately that it was just another inconvenience and she was resigned to her fate. Her thoughts turned to Barney. The man who had helped her through her recent struggles, but also the man who was the reason she was about to get shot.

He was standing next to her. The man with the gun had told him to move, so they were all huddled together. She turned and looked at him, and could detect a little smirk on his face. She wondered if he had finally gone crazy. Two days ago, he was in deep financial trouble, committed a sackable offence and was expecting to lose his job. Yesterday he had suddenly become a millionaire. One day later, before he has had a chance to spend a single penny of it, he was about to get killed. That would mess with anyone's mind. Take into account the two blows to the head he's endured recently and that could explain the strange reaction to the current situation they were now in. He reached out and held her hand, and his smirk turned into a broad grin. He seemed to be enjoying every minute. He didn't appear to be afraid in the slightest. That was because he had a feeling he wasn't going to get shot. Not today at least.

Liam on the other hand was deep in thought. Not his strongest attribute. He was trying to remember the next move. He'd done it many times before in his karate lessons. But this was different. This time there was no polite nodding of the heads and showing respect to each other before they entered combat. This man was holding a gun.

Meanwhile the gunman's young accomplice tried to get to his feet and was struggling. Barney had hurt him a lot more than they first thought. He let out a screech because of the sudden pain. The split-second distraction was just what Liam needed.

He sprang into action. In the blink of an eye, he had the man's arm twisted behind his back and the gun had fallen to the floor. Then he picked him up and smashed him down onto the floor with a sickening crunch. He lay motionless on the floor, and for a moment they wondered if he was still alive. But he started groaning and rubbing his arm, which didn't look good. Badly out of shape and for certain broken bones. Barney resisted kicking him. He looked hurt enough. The younger one said, 'Steve. Are you all right?'

To which he shouted, 'Don't use my name you stupid bastard.'

'Oh, sorry Mr Fletcher.'

'For fucks sake.'

Barney was right. These were a pair of amateurs.

Liam said, 'Fletcher? That's someone who makes barrels, isn't it?'

Mary, who had recovered her composure, corrected him.

'No, you dickhead. That's a cooper. A fletcher makes arrows.'

'That's handy,' said Barney. 'Maybe he can knock me up a new set of darts? I left mine on the train after the match last week. Someone in Worcestershire is probably using them right now in in a village pub.'

Liam said, 'I have an uncle called Cooper.'

The man they now knew as Steve Fletcher started shouting. 'What the hell are you talking about? I've broken my arm. Will someone call me an ambulance?'

Barney couldn't resist. 'That's a strange request at a time like this. But OK. You're an ambulance.'

Alison, who by now was finding the situation distasteful, told them, 'I think we should call an ambulance. And the police.'

But Barney told her, 'I don't really want to involve the police. We can sort this out ourselves.'

Alison couldn't accept that. 'Don't be ridiculous. He could have killed us!'

'Not with that gun he couldn't. Have you seen it? It's like something from the wild west. I think Wyatt Earp used one in the gunfight at the OK Corral.'

'Yes, and people died at the OK Corral.'

'That's because they used real guns.'

'Are you saying this one is a replica?'

'It's not even a replica. It's a kid's toy. It was probably part of a Cowboys and Indians set that they bought from 99p-Land or somewhere. I wouldn't be surprised if his mate over there gets a plastic bow and arrow out and points it at us.'

'I still think you need to call the police. And an ambulance.'

But Barney wasn't in a hurry to end their suffering. They'd made him suffer long enough and it was payback time. 'OK, let's call an ambulance. But it appears my phone battery is flat. How about yours Liam?'

Liam replied, 'I've no credit left. The screen says Emergency Calls Only.'

Steve Fletcher yelled, 'This is a fucking emergency!'

'Ooh temper temper,' said Barney. 'OK. I'll call an ambulance. Does anyone remember the number? I think it's got a 9 in it.'

'Liam said, 'Yes, it's 911. I've seen it on the TV, on those American crime dramas.'

Fletcher yelled again, '999!'

Mary joined in the fun, 'He must be concussed. He thinks he's a German now.'

Out of Order

Barney bent down and got up close to Fletcher's face.

'Listen carefully. Go back to your bosses and tell them this is the new deal. I'm going to pay you back three thousand pounds. I'm keeping the other half to cover damage to my car and to repair the window and door you've just smashed. And I need some compensation for your attack on me last week. That's the best offer you're going to get. Which isn't bad considering all the interest you've taken off me. You should advise them to accept it. I'll keep the police out of it in return for you never bothering me again. My circumstances have changed. I'm now in a position to cause you a lot of problems. And my friend here might just break your other arm. Do we have a deal?'

The man nodded.

'Not good enough!' said Barney. 'Say it out loud. Do we have a deal?'

'Yes. Now will you call me an ambulance. Quickly?'

'Oh dear. Some people just never learn. You're an ambulance quickly.'

Barney called 999 and the ambulance arrived 20 minutes later. The pair were taken off to hospital.

They sat around for another hour drinking more coffee, recovering from their ordeal. Then Liam and Mary left to go home. Alison stayed for a bit longer.

She said, 'Don't you think we should have called the police? I think they got off lightly.'

'You're probably right. But I haven't much faith in the British justice system. Liam and I would have probably been charged with GBH. And I wouldn't be surprised if I legally owed them that money. At least this way they don't get it all. This way it's all over at last. Besides, I'm a believer in rehabilitation. And we rehabilitated the shit out of them. That bloke's arm is not going to be much use to him for a long time, if ever. And as for the young lad, anyone who can be laid out by one punch from a wimp like me is hardly the heavy mob. There's clearly someone else running the business. These two are most likely just a pair of thugs on the payroll. In fact, I saw the people he works for a few mornings ago. They aren't very nice people. I don't want to inflame the situation. I don't know how far they will go, so giving them something will hopefully keep them away. And I'm also not keen on people like that finding out I'm now a millionaire.

'Do you know how we ended up in bed together?' Alison asked.

'No. But I suspect it was just for convenience, as the other two had grabbed the spare bed. I don't think there's any question of how they ended up in bed together.'

'How much else do you remember about last night?' she asked.

'I think all of it now. I'm still not too clear about the bit when I fainted. I remember talking to Colin, who was boring me to death. He left to go to the bar. Then Bowles was walking towards me. He was about to speak to me, then in the silence in a gap between songs I heard my phone make a noise. The next thing I remember is being picked up off the floor.

'Well let me fill in a few gaps for you. First of all, I shouted at

Richard and called him a heartless bastard. So, it might be me he wants to get rid of next. And then when you fainted, and were lying on the floor, you asked me if I would marry you.'

'Wow! I'd forgotten all about it.'

After a few minutes silence he said, 'So how did you react to that?'

'I told you not to be so bloody ridiculous, and suggested you must have landed on your head when you fell.'

'Oh. I see.' His words were filled with disappointment.

'But that was before I knew you'd won the lottery.'

'You're not trying to tell me you'd have given a different answer just because I'd won two million quid?'

'Mmm. Who knows? Maybe I would have. I couldn't be married to someone as loopy as you without having some kind of financial compensation.'

'I suppose not. Flatterer.'

'I got married once because I was in love. Look how that worked out. If ever I am foolish enough to get married again it will be to some rich mug who I can boss around and spend all his money.'

There was another long silent pause.

'Then will you?'

'Yes.'

35

The day that everybody who plays the lottery dreams of had arrived for Barney. The moment when you can swagger into the office tell your boss to shove his job.

He was still in a state of shock from the events of the weekend. He had told himself to behave calmly and dignified, but he was going to enjoy the moment.

He arrived in Winchester at ten o'clock on Monday morning after being stuck in a traffic jam on the motorway. Something that he wouldn't need to do ever again if he didn't want to. As he walked through the office, he said hello as he passed several people he knew. They looked puzzled to see him there. Most had heard rumours he'd been sacked. Others had heard a different story.

He knocked on the door of Richard Bowles office.

'Ah, come in Cecil. I've been expecting you.'

'Why? I never told you I was coming.'

'I know. But I had a feeling you'd be coming here. Congratulations on your lottery win.'

This threw Barney off balance a bit. And also took away some of the fun he was expecting to have.

'How did you know?'

'You should know by now you can't keep any secrets in this

place.'

'Yes. Very true.'

'I suppose you've come to tell me what to do with the job?'

'That was my intention. But you've kind of spoilt it a bit.'

'Sorry about that. You still can do that of course. But first I'd like to explain something about Saturday night. How well do you know the operator Alison?'

'You mean my fiancée? Reasonably well.'

Richard was silent for a moment. Then gave a little smile.

'You are full of surprises. That piece of gossip hasn't circulated yet. That would explain her verbal attack on me on Saturday night.'

'Well, no, it wouldn't,' said Barney. 'We didn't get engaged until Sunday. We weren't even a couple on Saturday.'

'Oh. I see. I think. You'll be pleased to know she did a fine job of sticking up for you. I suppose that means we'll be losing her too now?'

'Maybe not straight away. She loves her job, so you might have her for a bit longer. Neither of us have decided what our plans are yet. Why did you ask how well I knew her?'

'It's just that the reason she had a big go at me was because she thought you'd fainted because I fired you. She obviously didn't know at that point that you'd fainted because you'd just received the news that you'd won the lottery. Whatever you think of me, I wouldn't fire someone at a Christmas party. Besides, I had no grounds to sack you at that point.'

'So why did you come over to me?'

'I make a point of trying to talk to all my staff at social gatherings. I couldn't leave you out. That would make me look petty. Besides, at that point I had no idea what you'd done on Friday. I'd gone home early and didn't answer my phone. I only found out this morning that you'd told one of our valued customers to shove his cock into a cup of hot coffee.'

'That's not true.'

'Isn't it?'

'No. I said knob, not cock.'

'Oh, that's alright then. That technicality will make a big difference to your defence. And I'm not too pleased that you referred to me as a bellend.'

Barney felt slightly embarrassed, and for some bizarre reason felt he was in a weaker position than usual. As if he had less power, now that he had lots of it. As if there was no reason to put up a fight.

'Sorry about that. Did you manage to placate him?'

'Yes, I did, eventually. I'm an expert in that. Mainly thanks to you I've had a lot of practice. But it was very difficult. I was trying desperately not to laugh when he was describing what you said. It's a good job he couldn't see my face.'

Barney was pleased to see this other side of him, and had some sympathy. It can be very painful when you're trying not to laugh. His recent exploits with Wan Ki, cartoon mouse voice, and farty lady in the fried chicken restaurant sprang to mind. He was pleasantly surprised to hear him revealing he had at least a little bit of a sense of humour.

Out of Order

But Barney hadn't come all this way to make friends with his long-standing enemy. He wanted a dust up of some kind.

'I know it doesn't matter anymore, but why do you always take the side of the customer? You don't stick up for your staff. We have a right to carry out our jobs without suffering verbal abuse or ridicule.'

'To be fair, I could hardly defend you in this case.'

'Maybe not. But you don't in any case.'

'My wife told me the same thing. But it's not true. I'm always sticking up for my staff. It's just that I have to do it in a different way. If I hadn't apologised for your behaviour on numerous occasions, just think how many customers could have cancelled the contract and moved to a different vending supplier. Our jobs all depend on the number of customers we have. We have to try and keep them happy, no matter how obnoxious they are.'

Although Barney didn't entirely agree with him, he hadn't seen things from this point of view before, and kind of understood it. It seems we live in a world where businesses have to do whatever is required to succeed, no matter if its morally right or wrong.

'So, may I ask, if I hadn't won the money and wasn't in a position to resign, would you have given me the sack this morning?'

'Yes. You wouldn't have left me any choice. If you'd have got away with that, you would think you could get away with anything. The results would have been devastating.'

Barney resented that remark. 'I'm not as bad as you think. I only treat people the way they treat me. I never start it.'

'Hmm. If you say so. I very much doubt that is always the case. So, what happens now. Do you prefer to be fired, or would you rather resign?'

'If I resign, do I have to work my months' notice?'

'You must be fucking joking! Do you seriously think I'd let you go running around out there if you didn't have any worries about losing your job? It would be carnage.'

'In that case I'll leave it to you. Would you like the pleasure of firing me?'

Bowles waited. It was so tempting to say the words he'd been wanting to for a long time. But he didn't. Instead, he said, 'I accept your resignation. It's been... interesting working with you. I would say goodbye and good luck, but I think you've already had your share of good luck. So, goodbye.'

Then they shook hands.

'Can I ask you one more thing before you leave?'

'Fire away.'

'Will you finally admit that it was you I saw on the television, throwing the ball back at the Oval? The day when coincidentally I refused to give you a holiday when you told me you wanted a day off to go to the Oval?'

'No, as I told you at the time, that must have been someone who looked a little bit like me. I was at home, sick.'

'He didn't look a little bit like you. He looked exactly like you. And according to Mary, he was wearing one of your tee shirts.'

'We've already discovered how unreliable Mary's information can be.'

'Was she wrong about the tee shirt?'

'No, she was right. I was surprised when I heard that too. What a coincidence.'

'And unless I'm very much mistaken, the man sitting next to you was your dad.'

'How do you know what my dad looks like?'

'I didn't. But I do now. When you requested the holiday, you said you wanted to take your dad to the cricket as a 70th birthday present.'

'Oh that. Yes, I believe he still went without me. In fact, I think he went with my identical twin brother instead. That reminds me. I must get back that tee shirt he borrowed off me.'

'I can see why our customers get wound up by you.'

'Why did you refuse me the day off in the first place? Did you have genuine reasons, or was it just out of spite?'

'No, no. I had genuine reasons. Almost as genuine as your mysterious illness.'

Barney left his office having had a totally different showdown to what he'd been anticipating. He said goodbye to everyone and left the office. He hoped to see some of them at the wedding, wherever and whenever that would be. He would be back to Winchester in a month to bring the car back. Richard said he could keep the car for a month. He hardly needed it. He could buy any car he wanted now. But he didn't want to appear ungrateful.

He walked out of the office, feeling quite sad. He'd been doing this job for twenty-two years, and at this company for twelve of them. He was remembering some of the good times he'd had, and was forgetting having to get out of bed on a cold January morning to sit in a traffic jam. He really must have still been in shock.

On the way home he was wondering why he felt so down. His dreams had come true. He wouldn't have loan sharks threatening him. He could buy whatever he wanted. He could go wherever he wanted. He could buy a bigger house, in a nicer location. He could improve the lives of friends and relatives. He was going to get married. He would eventually sit down and make some plans. But his first concern was finding something to do this afternoon.

36

Eight months had passed since that eventful Christmas party weekend. Even though she was married to a millionaire, Alison was still working, but she wouldn't be for much longer. Soon she would be off on maternity leave and was unlikely to return. She was in the depot loading up the van and went to tell Mary the news of her pregnancy. Mary gave her a big hug.

'Well, congratu-fucking-lations! So, you and Barney finally worked out how to take your clothes off before you got into bed.'

The rest of the office staff laughed. Alison wondered briefly why they all knew what she meant. But she had worked out some time ago that most of the office gossip was started by Mary. After all it was thanks to Mary's false information that she had shouted at Richard at the Christmas party. Something for which he had forgiven her. In fact, Richard seemed to be a completely different character these days. He was much easier going and less stressed out since Barney had left.

Even though she quite liked her job, Barney had been exaggerating somewhat when he told Richard she loved it. She had continued working, mainly because everything happened so quickly and she was still coming to terms with it all. Work provided some continuity. She had made the decision to quit working once she'd had the baby. They were buying a new house and life would never be the same again. But for a little while longer she was going to continue filling spirals with packets of crisps and bars of chocolate.

Alison and Barney got married on a beach in the Seychelles. There were no guests. This was chiefly Barney's suggestion. Alison didn't have any relatives, and she had only just started to reconnect with her old friends that she'd lost touch with due to her bullying ex-husband, so if any guests were invited, they would all be on Barney's side. He didn't feel comfortable with that, and besides she loved the idea of going to the Seychelles.

When they got back home, they had a party to which everyone was invited. Barney's parents were there, but managed to avoid each other for most of the evening. There was quite a large contingency from Vendetta, and of course all of the darts team. Alison had managed to get three of her old friends and their husbands along.

The song they chose for the first dance was Every Day is a Winding Road by Sheryl Crow. Not the normal tempo for a first dance at a wedding. It was more of a joke between the two of them. The opening line of the song is 'I hitched a ride with a vending machine repair man'. Barney also liked the line about the vending machine repair man being 'high on intellectualism'. In your face, Red Dwarf! It wasn't a smoochy song, so they just jumped around to it until everybody else joined in.

Later in the evening he was chatting with Daffy. Daffy was commenting on his choice of first dance.

'I'm a fan of Cheryl Crow. Did you know she did a brilliant cover of Led Zeppelin's Rock and Roll? In my opinion it was even better than the original.'

This brought back some mixed memories for Barney. Mainly happy ones.

'I must confess I don't know the original all that well. I've listened to it out of curiosity, because a few years ago I almost had to sing it in front of a crowd. I don't think my version would have sounded as good as Cheryl Crow's. Or Led Zeppelin's for that matter.'

Spurred on by his wave of nostalgia, and of course plenty of lager, Barney came up with an idea. He had to make a speech anyway, thanking various people and other formalities, and at the end he mentioned that there were two other songs which in a tenuous way had played some part in getting Alison and him together. He asked the DJ to play Rock and Roll by Led Zeppelin and to everyone's surprise and amusement he kept hold of the microphone and sang along to it. It didn't sound as bad as a Karaoke because the vocals of Robert Plant helped him disguise his voice, and most of the bewildered guests joined in too, many of them headbanging on the dance floor and suddenly the place was rocking, but he blasted it out with such fervour it was bad enough to sound good.

Alison came up to him when he'd finished and kissed him. There were tears in her 'perfectly healthy' eyes.

'You're mad! I hope you don't expect me to sing I Will Survive?'

'No. But it would be appropriate after all you've been through. If ever that song was written for anyone, it was you.'

Alison thought that was possibly the nicest thing anyone had ever said to her. Certainly, with sincerity at least. She knew there was some truth in it too.

She said, 'Don't be so soppy. It doesn't suit you.'

Barney laughed.

'By the way, what am I going to call you now?' asked Alison.

'What do you mean?'

'Well, I can't call you Barney.'

'Why not?'

'Because I'm a Barney too now. And I can hardly call you Cecil. You hate being called Cecil.'

'I'll have to think about that one Mrs Barney.'

Mary and Liam were continuing to have some kind of relationship, despite everyone who worked with them saying it wouldn't last. Barney had given Liam ten thousand pounds. He deserved it for sorting out the man with the gun, even though it was fake. Liam claims he didn't know it was fake at the time, and that was no doubt true, given Liam's power of deduction. Barney had decided to give all of his close friends ten thousand pounds, but that didn't cost him much. Apart from Liam, all his friends were in the darts team and they were all millionaires themselves now.

The darts team didn't have their match in Las Vegas like they used to talk about when they had only dreamed of winning the lottery, but instead went to the Netherlands. Darts is very popular over there, and they found a team on a website who were happy to accommodate them. They had one night in a little village where the darts took place, then spent two more nights in Amsterdam to have a proper celebration.

Roy, Daffy, and Fiona had all quit their jobs. Tom and Joe were still working. The team were all in agreement to keep on playing. They had now stopped for the summer, but had continued playing after Christmas until the end of the season in April. They still played the lottery leg just out of habit.

Alison came along to two matches despite being reluctant at first.

'I don't know much about darts,' she protested.

Barney told her, 'Neither does anybody else. Three arrows and a board. It's hardly rocket science. Besides, the darts match is just an excuse. It's about meeting friends and having a drink. So, she was persuaded to give it a try and enjoyed it very much. The team were most welcoming to her, and had since become good friends with some of them.

Barney hadn't done too much since his retirement, apart from getting married. He'd bought a decent new car after he returned the company one, but he hadn't spent much of the money yet. He certainly would do, but was taking his time planning his future. He had given his mum and his dad a hundred thousand pounds each. He'd had a few more trips to the lake district to visit his mum, and met up with his dad a few times to watch England test matches in the pub. His dad would say, 'I suppose you won't need to scrounge any more money off me now that you're rich?'

To which Barney would say, 'Why do you think I gave you the hundred grand? It's so I can sponge it back off you when I've spent all mine.'

Today he was wandering around the high street and popped in to the Cross Keys for a pint, and to watch a bit of cricket. While he was in there Liam phoned.

'Alright Barney? Are you busy?'

'Nah. I'm just having a pint and watching the test match.'

'It's alright for some. Listen, I'm having trouble fixing one of those Cafeblam 73s. I need your help.'

'You can't have my help. I've retired. I stopped working there eight months ago. Remember?'

'I don't mean come and physically help me. I just want some advice.'

Barney sighed loudly so Liam could hear. But secretly he was quite pleased. He'd missed this. 'OK. What's the problem?'

'The screen says "Out of service. Error code 12". I don't know how to clear it.'

'Turn the power off and back on again.'

Liam turned the power off and back on again. Then there was a spell of silence. Barney waited in anticipation.

'Yes. That seems to have worked. Thanks.'

Barney laughed. Liam was handy to have around when he needed someone to dish out a few karate chops to yobs pointing guns at him, demanding money, but his engineering skills were somewhat limited. He returned to his pint of lager. Although he'd missed having these conversations with Liam, and the inevitable drink after they had done a job together, he was still happy not to be working. Except for one thing. He missed the conversations with stubborn customers and the ones he could make look stupid. He found himself longing for one of those ridiculous verbal dust-ups. His wish was soon to be granted.

He left the pub and was feeling hungry. He spotted a fried chicken takeaway. Just what he needed. Chicken and chips. The food of millionaires. He entered the shop and was served by a spotty teenager. He was having flashbacks to his Torquay nightmare, and was relieved to see that none of the spots were yellow.

'Hello, what would you like?'

'Two pieces of fried chicken and chips please.'

'Would you like that as a meal?'

'Well what else would I do with it?'

'No, I mean would you like it as a meal deal. It works out cheaper.'

'Alright. We'll call it a meal deal.'

'That'll be £3.95. What drink would you like?'

'I don't really want a drink.'

'If you don't have a drink it will no longer be a meal deal. It will cost £4.50.'

'In that case I'll have a bottle of water.'

'Bottles are not included in the meal deal. Only drinks from the pumps.'

'Give me a Coke then.'

'Diet or ordinary?'

'It really doesn't matter which one you give me. I've got no intention of drinking it. I don't like Coke. I'll be throwing it away when I get outside.'

'Isn't that a bit of a waste?'

'I would say so. A waste that could be easily avoided by you just not pouring the Coke.'

'I don't make the rules. I just work here. Here's your meal. Have a nice day.'

'I'll try to. I don't suppose you would throw this Coke away for me? On second thoughts, don't answer that.'

Epilogue

Twenty-Five Years Later

It was two days after Barney's 70th birthday. To celebrate he'd arranged a day out at Aintree to watch the Grand National, just like he always said he would. Despite being still enormously rich he didn't splash out on an expensive hospitality box. He just wanted to mix with the ordinary punters. He still considered himself an ordinary punter. He was happy to drink pints of lager, although Alison and Mary were on the champagne, and they were wearing ridiculously large and expensive hats. Mary still worked for Vendetta, but was retiring at the end of the year. Liam was working in a gym at a leisure centre. That was much more enjoyable for him. He had given up on engineering many years ago. Without Barney's help he'd struggled with his work, so decided it would be better to move on and try something new. They never got married, but they had a son Louis who was now 23, a year younger than Jack, who was Barney and Alison's son.

Louis and Jack had wandered off on their own. They didn't want to hang around with the oldies. Barney and Jack had just had an angry exchange before he went off. Barney said to Alison, 'What's the matter with that miserable sod? He could start an argument in an empty room.'

'I think we all know who he gets that from, don't we?'

Jack was a real mummy's boy. He could do no wrong in her

eyes.

Roy, Tom, Daffy, and Fiona from the darts team were all there. The only one missing from the old gang was Joe, who they'd lost touch with. The team didn't play in a league any more, but met up at least once a year, somewhere different each time, like Dublin, or Edinburgh for a game of darts and a curry. They still hadn't made it to Las Vegas, but talked about it every year. Maybe they'll do it next year. Barney had tried playing for a village pub team in the Lake District, but he soon gave up. It was never as enjoyable as the Mickey Mouse Club.

Barney and Alison had bought a lovely house in the Lake District. It gave him the opportunity to tick off the rest of the 197 tarn dippings. His mum who was now 92 still lived there, but didn't run the B&B any longer. His dad had died nine years ago. Barney would have liked him to be there. He was there when he had come up with the original idea of going to the Grand National.

They were all getting drunker, louder, and sillier. That was why Louis and Jack had gone off on their own. They knew their parents were going to behave like big kids and embarrass them. They'd seen it often enough. They all went to place some bets.

Mary said to Barney, 'Do you remember that time we went to Windsor races?'

'Yes, I remember it well. You had a bit more success than me.'

'I suppose you're going to point out that the Grand National has thirty big fences I've got to take into consideration?'

'Not really. They've made the fences so small thanks to animal rights protesters that it might as well be a flat race these days. Have you picked a horse yet?'

'Yes. There's one called Laughing Louis. That has to be the one.'

'But it's 66-1. It's got no chance.'

'Bollocks to you! You told me Magnificent Mary had no chance at Windsor and she won at 12-1. I took no fucking notice of you then, and I'm taking no fucking notice of you now.'

That was more like the old Mary. She'd cut out the swearing when Louis was around, but now that he'd gone off, she could really let rip.

Barney was suddenly feeling quite overwhelmed and wandered off on his own for a while. He was reflecting on how his life had gone. He'd made it to seventy. He didn't think the money had changed him too much over the years. He still had a strong sense of what was right and what was wrong. And how people should treat each other.

He was thinking about his friends. Thinking about how great it was that Liam and Mary had stayed friends with them for all these years. The same goes for the darts team. They had known each other for so long and were growing old together. The millions of pounds had been more than handy, but his friends were far more valuable to him.

Alison caught up with him.

'What's up with you, you soppy sod?'

'Nothing. The wind is making my eyes water.'

She hugged him and they stayed like that for a while. She remembered the first time they hugged. It was in a hospital just after she'd been given the news that she wasn't going to lose her eyesight. He could be difficult to live with at times. Always sounding off about something. But thanks to him she had the thing she wanted more than anything. Her son was the most important thing in her life.

'Come on. Let's go and get another drink,' they both said at the same time.

They went back to join the others and they all wandered off to find a different bar. They came across a bar which had a row of three coffee machines with the Vendetta logo.

'Look!' Shouted Mary. 'They've got our fucking machines!'

'Yes. They're Vendetta alright. Two of them have 'Out of Order' signs on them. Shall I go and fix them?' said Barney, by now very drunk.

Liam chipped in, 'You wouldn't stand a chance mate. Those things have changed so much since you retired. Let me show you'

Liam approached the one working machine and said to it, 'Hello'

The machine spoke back to him.

'Hello Liam. You are no longer employed by Vendetta. I cannot give you access to my program. High consumption of alcohol detected. Please take extra when handling hot drinks. Would you like to purchase a drink?'

'No.'

'Thank you. Goodbye.'

Mary said, 'Allow me. Hello coffee machine.'

It replied, 'Hello Mary. Vendetta employee. High consumption of alcohol detected. Please take extra care when handling hot drinks. Have you come to refill me?'

She said, 'No I haven't. Piss off!'

The machine said, 'Would you like to purchase a drink?'

'No, I fucking wouldn't.'

'There's no need to be like that. Goodbye.'

A giggling Alison said, 'Let me have a try. Hello Mr coffee machine. Or are you a Mrs?'

It spoke back to her. 'Voice not recognised. High consumption of alcohol detected. Please take extra care when handling hot drinks. Would you like to purchase a drink?'

Alison had left Vendetta before the voice recognition system was used. She was disappointed the machine didn't know her.

'No, I wouldn't. And you're very rude. How dare you not recognise me? I was refilling coffee machines before you were born.'

The machine said, 'Thank you. Goodbye.'

How can it tell we're pissed?' asked Barney.

'Don't ask me,' replied Liam. 'I never really understood how vending machines worked I just blagged my way through the job for years.'

Alison and Mary were getting giggly and they had a laugh at a toff in a top hat ordering champagne at the bar. Mary said, 'When I was a kid, I had an aunt who thought she was posh. I used to think she was swearing when she was asking if people wanted coffee or tea. She'd say "Anyone fuckoffy? Or who's fartee?" It was shocking for a little girl to hear. I don't like bad language.' They both burst into another fit of giggles.

Listening to Mary talking about her posh aunt gave Barney an idea. He wanted to have a go with the machine. He put on a ludicrously fake posh voice.

'Good ahhhfternoon my good coffee machine. This is King William speaking. Ay say, dooo tell me. Could one hev a china cup full of your finest cappuccino, with gold sprinkles?'

The machine started the reply with, 'Voice not recognised. High consumption of alcohol detected. Please take extra care when handling hot drinks. Sorry. You are not King William…'

But then another angry voice cut in.

'Would you mind not messing around with the machine? It is the only one working and there are people waiting to use it.'

Barney turned around and saw a queue of people impatiently

watching him.

'Oops. Sorry.'

He stepped aside and allowed a woman to approach the machine. She put her finger on a pad. The machine said, 'Fingerprint recognised. Welcome back Sarah. Would you like your usual drink?'

'Yes please?'

'Your drink may include ingredients which may cause mild irritation, serious illness or death. Would you like to continue?'

'Yes.'

The machine dispensed a cup of coffee.

'Fourteen pounds and sixty pence will be deducted from your bank account. Thank you for using me. Would you like to take part in a brief questionnaire rating your satisfaction with your beverage experience?'

Sarah ignored that and walked away with her drink.

They were about to walk back to the racetrack just as an engineer in a Vendetta uniform turned up to repair the two machines. The machine the engineer started to work on recognised the voice and said a name. Mary and Liam introduced themselves to the engineer and they chatted for a while.

Barney stayed in the background. He didn't need to introduce himself. The engineer already knew him. She broke off her conversation with the other two and spoke to Barney in a Liverpool accent he recognised all too well. She was now 62, but still as good looking, or even better than she was twenty-five years ago.

'Hello. Remember me?'

'Yes, I do,' he replied, hoping she wouldn't say anything that would embarrass him. 'I believe we were training together in Torquay?'

'Yes. That's right,' she said, with a suggestive tone in her voice. 'How could I forget?'

'I'm glad to see you were successful in your bid to become an engineer. You must be a good one too if you're still at it all these years later. That must have been enjoyable proving your boss wrong.'

'It was. And not only that, after he retired, I was promoted. I've been a senior engineer for just over eleven years. Helping other engineers with problems they can't solve. And there are two other female engineers working at our place now.'

Alison could sense there was some sort of history between the two of them and started to feel a touch of jealousy. So, she stepped in to interrupt the conversation, 'Aren't you going to introduce us?'

'Of course. This is my wife Alison. And this is... Err'

The coffee machine had just announced her name. But Barney didn't quite catch it.

Available worldwide from
Amazon and all good bookstores

---

www.mtp.agency

www.facebook.com/mtp.agency

@mtp_agency

Michael Terence Publishing

www.ingramcontent.com/pod-product-compliance
Lightning Source LLC
LaVergne TN
LVHW091533060526
838200LV00036B/593